"I'm sorry, Sop[hie]," Alexander said

Sophie was not pleased to receive his apology. "For kissing me?" she demanded.

"No! How could I be sorry for something that gave me more pleasure than I imagined possible?"

This statement found even less favor. Why should Alexander feel so surprised? Was it beyond the bounds of possibility that kissing Sophie Gordon could be such a pleasurable pastime?

"What exactly are you sorry for then?" she asked.

Alexander captured her hands. "Because we were interrupted. Because I gave in to the urge to make love to you in just about the most uncomfortable place possible. And because," he went on, his voice husky, "I've known you for so long—and never dreamed so much fire lay hidden behind that disciplined exterior of yours...."

CATHERINE GEORGE was born in Wales, and following her marriage to an engineer, lived eight years in Brazil at a gold mine site, an experience she would later draw upon for her books. It was not until she and her husband returned to England and bought a village post office and general store that she submitted her first book at her husband's encouragement. Now her husband helps manage their household so that Catherine can devote more time to her writing. They have two children, a daughter and a son, who share their mother's love of language and writing.

Books by Catherine George

HARLEQUIN PRESENTS
873—SILENT CRESCENDO
992—THE MARRIAGE BED
1016—LOVE LIES SLEEPING
1065—TOUCH ME IN THE MORNING
1152—VILLAIN OF THE PIECE
1184—TRUE PARADISE

HARLEQUIN ROMANCE
2535—RELUCTANT PARAGON
2571—DREAM OF MIDSUMMER
2720—DESIRABLE PROPERTY
2822—THE FOLLY OF LOVING
2924—MAN OF IRON
2942—THIS TIME ROUND

CATHERINE GEORGE

loveknot

Harlequin Books

TORONTO • NEW YORK • LONDON
AMSTERDAM • PARIS • SYDNEY • HAMBURG
STOCKHOLM • ATHENS • TOKYO • MILAN

Harlequin Presents first edition December 1989
ISBN 0-373-11225-4

Original hardcover edition published in 1988
by Mills & Boon Limited

CHAPTER ONE

THE crowded room simmered with tension. Eyes met eyes and slid away, and conversation diminished to embarrassed murmurs of conjecture as the wedding guests, far too many of them for comfort in the close confines of the register office, waited for the bride. The registrar's smile grew fixed and finally disappeared as he darted pointed looks at the clock on the wall, his occasional dry cough adding to the susurration of whispers and shuffling feet from those gathered together to witness the joining in marriage of Miss Delphine Wyndham and Mr Alexander Paget.

Alone in a sea of unrest, the bridegroom sat like a rock.

And had done for half an hour, thought Sophie Gordon, as the clock on the town hall chimed in confirmation. And Alexander had never fidgeted once. The sunlit room was stiflingly hot, but every sleek, fair hair on his head lay in place, his white collar pristine above the dark morning-coat, the gardenia in his lapel as fresh as the moment he'd arrived. Alexander, as Sophie knew better than most, aimed as nearly as possible for perfection in all things, which made it all the more unbelievable that Delphine dared flout his well-known views on punctuality.

No man, surely, deserved to wait so long—and so publicly—for his bride to put in an appearance. Sophie was startled by a sudden pang of compassion. Of all the feelings she had harboured for Alexander Paget over the years, compassion was certainly a first, in spite of the links between them. Owing to the friendship between their respective parents he had inevitably been around all her life, sometimes in the background, occasionally to the fore. Once, briefly, she had even agonised in the throes of puppy-love over him. That, at least, had died a natural death from sheer under-nourishment, she thought, amused. Alexander had been so insufferably superior in his college days that her teenage adoration had soon veered in other directions.

Alexander played a prominent enough role in her life currently, it was true, because for the past few years she had been his secretary. A very good one, too, in her own opinion. Only a wife knew a man better than his confidential secretary, and in her own case, reflected Sophie, probably not nearly so well.

Sophie stole a glance up at her father to find him eyeing the bride's mother with professional concern. The lady sat twisting her doeskin gloves into ruin, her face deeply flushed beneath the brim of her hat.

'Hypertensive,' murmured Dr Gordon, *sotto voce*.

'Hardly surprising,' answered his daughter in kind, brows raised as she caught the eye of Edward Peregrine Paget, cousin and best man to the bridegroom. Perry kept twisting round in his seat to

look towards the door, as if he hoped the bride
might have materialised there when his back was
turned. Fat chance, thought Sophie. When
Delphine Wyndham makes her entry not a soul will
be left in doubt.

When, at long last, the door did open, all heads
but one swivelled as if jerked by the same string.
But expectancy changed to surprise as, in place of
the bride, her father stood in the doorway,
beckoning urgently to Perry, who nudged
Alexander and went with him from the room,
closing the door on the buzz of comment which
broke out an all sides. Mrs Wyndham sagged
against the relative seated next to her, and Kate
Paget, Alexander's stepmother, turned round to
the Gordons, her attractive face worried.

'Something wrong, do you think, David?'

Dr Gordon smiled reassuringly. 'Delphine's
probably held up in the traffic.'

Or she's broken a fingernail, or laddered a
stocking, thought Sophie without charity.
Delphine Wyndham would think nothing of
keeping a room full of people waiting while the
vital adjustment was made.

While the guests waited speculation very plainly
ran riot through the room, some of it anxious,
some of the faces agog with an avid curiosity,
Sophie noted with disgust. She felt most concerned
for Kate Paget, who tensed visibly as Alexander
and Perry came back into the room. The bridegroom spoke privately with the registrar, then
turned to face the assembled company, his green
eyes frozen in his good-looking face.

'I apologise to you all for the long wait,' he said with courtesy. 'I regret that there will be no wedding ceremony after all. Delphine, I am told, has changed her mind.'

There was a piercing wail as Mrs Wyndham collapsed in the arms of her companion, and Dr Gordon sprang up at once to assist, Kate Paget close behind him. It took some time to restore the distraught woman to some semblance of composure, while the deserted bridegroom waited, immobile, his face devoid of emotion. Sophie stayed in her seat, well out of the way, pitying Alexander from the bottom of her heart. All this would be so horribly novel for him. He was accustomed to a life amazingly free of the trials and tribulations other, lesser beings had to bear. She viewed him dispassionately, trying to see him with the eyes of a stranger. He was a very fit, attractive specimen of his sex, she conceded; tallish, slim, muscular, with thick, sleek hair only a little darker than the flaxen fairness of his youth. Nor were his assets confined to the physical. A successful architect in a respected firm established by his grandfather in the town of Deansbury, Alexander had a name and professional reputation known to everyone. Sophie found it hard to credit that even Delphine could have been so heartless as to leave a man like Alexander at the altar. Not, of course, that the table in the register office was anything like an altar, in spite of the flowers someone had arranged so tastefully. But the principle was the same. Wherever a jilted bridegroom was left could only be described as the lurch.

After the weeping Mrs Wyndham had finally been escorted from the room by her nearest and dearest, Alexander turned once more to the remaining guests.

'Although the wedding itself has been cancelled, a perfectly good meal is waiting to be eaten at the Deansbury Country Club, as arranged.' He smiled very slightly, beginning, at last, to show visible signs of strain. 'Forgive me if I make myself scarce. Under the circumstances I could only be the spectre at the feast. Perry here will take over for me, and on behalf of Mr Wyndham and his wife I urge you all to take advantage of their hospitality.'

'It was quite horrible,' Sophie told her grandmother over lunch next day. 'I never dreamed I could feel so sorry for Alexander.'

'Why not?' asked Cecily Wainwright with interest.

Sophie thought for a moment. 'Well, you know Alexander, Gran. He never seems in need of sympathy, let alone pity. He forges through life without a hitch. Even I can appreciate what a good catch he is for a girl—clever, successful, plenty of money——'

'Not to mention extremely attractive,' added her grandmother. 'Delphine Wyndham's reasons for crying off must have been very powerful.'

'Greed, I suppose.'

'And incredibly bad taste if she went off with that Foyle person.'

'Ah, but Terry Foyle is Delphine's Dr Frankenstein, Gran.' Sophie grinned wickedly.

Mrs Wainwright wagged an admonishing finger, but agreed there was truth in what Sophie said. Without Terry Foyle's consummate skill with a camera, Delphine Wyndham's rise to top modelling fame would never have been so meteoric, in spite of her looks and amazing waist-length black hair. The dynamic little East-Ender had transformed mere prettiness into every man's dream of erotic beauty, resulting in an offer from an American cosmetics firm to the pair as a package, a contract Terry Foyle had come chasing hotfoot to Deansbury to wave in front of Delphine's nose at the eleventh hour on the very day of the wedding.

'No contest,' said Sophie. 'Alexander and Deansbury had no chance against Terry Foyle and the Dreamgirl Corporation of LA.'

'So Delphine's flown off to the City of the Angels—most inappropriate.' Mrs Wainwright looked at Sophie questioningly. 'And how is Alexander?'

'Bearing up with fortitude.' Sophie's eyes danced as she told her grandmother how the jilted bridegroom had actually gone off to Greece after all, just as originally planned for his honeymoon. His passion for ancient ruins would be indulged to the full, even if those of the flesh were likely to go unfulfilled.

'Sophie!' Mrs Wainwright tried hard to look shocked, but was evidently much struck by Alexander's practical outlook. 'But surely not at the honeymoon hotel!'

'Oh, yes. Alexander was quite unshakeable

about it, according to Aunt Kate.'

Mrs Wainwright applauded his common sense, and reiterated her scorn for any woman addle-brained enough to desert such a level-headed bridegroom. Sophie, on the other hand, looked forward to Alexander's eventual return to Deansbury with mixed feelings, certain his mood was bound to be black in the extreme.

'Delphine's so gorgeous,' she said with gloom. 'Alexander's bound to be like a bear with a sore head when he gets back to work. Though why he imagined a girl like that would settle down to connubial bliss in Deansbury I'll never know.'

'Probably he just hoped she would, darling. Men can be very naïve in some ways.'

'Naïve! Alexander?' Sophie hooted. 'He's the shrewdest man I know. Delphine must be the one miscalculation he's ever made in his life.'

The two women went out into the garden after lunch to enjoy their coffee in the sunshine and catch up on family news. Both of them looked forward to their fortnightly lunches together. Sophie, in particular, relished the peace and quiet of the comfortable house where her mother had grown up, enjoying the contrast to her life at home. Here at Greenacre she could almost revert to carefree childhood again, whereas in Deansbury she ran the Gordon household and looked after her father and brothers in the time left over from her job with Paget & Son, Chartered Architects.

'When are the twins getting back from France?' asked Mrs Wainwright.

'Wednesday, I think.'

'Whereupon you, I assume, will be presented with a lovingly hoarded supply of dirty laundry.'

Sophie laughed. 'I'd prefer that to endless name tapes. Before they take off for Edinburgh I've got dozens of the wretched things to sew on.'

'I hope the university knows what it has in store,' commented Mrs Wainwright, and cast a keen look in her grandchild's direction. 'And what will you do with yourself then?'

Sophie looked startled. 'Do?'

'Now Tim has gone out to herd sheep in Australia, and Mark and Matthew will soon be setting Edinburgh alight, it seems to me that your presence in your father's house is not as essential as once it was.'

The thought was by no means new to Sophie. It had never left her over the past months. But apart from less food and laundry to cope with she foresaw very little change in her life. There was still her father to consider. And as a doctor David Gordon relied on her more than other fathers might have done in their particular circumstances, if only because he needed her in the house to answer the telephone on the two nights a week he was on call. When she said as much Mrs Wainwright looked disapproving.

'Don't you ever long for a life of your own, Sophie? I can't help feeling Louise would be up in arms if she could see the trend your life has taken lately.'

Louise Gordon had gone off by coach on a Christmas shopping trip to London shortly after Sophie's sixteenth birthday. The coach had crashed in fog in a pile-up on the motorway, and David Gordon and his four children had been left without the mainstay of their lives. Louise's father had suffered a stroke at the news and Cecily Wainwright had been torn apart by her loyalties to both her stricken husband and her grandchildren, forced to stand by while Sophie, the eldest, changed overnight from a carefree schoolgirl into housekeeper and surrogate mother to her brothers, studying for her A-level examinations and subsequent secretarial course at the same time as learning to manage the household. Dr Gordon had employed a woman to help clean the house in the beginning, but when the lady eventually retired Sophie elected to manage alone, since by that time Tim was away in Cirencester at Agricultural College, and Mark and Matthew old enough to help a little. And, if sometimes she longed passionately for solitude and privacy, only Cecily Wainwright ever really knew how much.

'I think it's high time you left the nest yourself,' the latter said trenchantly.

'Oh, so do I,' Sophie agreed, 'but I can't just take off and leave Dad. Besides, where would I go?'

Before Cecily Wainwright could make any suggestions the telephone rang, and she went off to answer it, leaving Sophie to her daydream of a place of her own. Somewhere, anywhere, just so long as it had no importunate men demanding food and clean shirts when all she longed for was time to herself after her daily stint at Paget & Son. She loved her father—and her brothers; felt closer to them than most girls perhaps, due to their particular situation. But secretly she hankered after space and time to herself. And the latter was slipping by. Almost twenty-four years of her life had been spent within the confines of Deansbury and the family circle. Even her job had been tailor-made for her, decided for her by others. The moment her secretarial course was completed Alexander had been conveniently in need of a secretary and that had been that. She was handed over to him like a parcel, and everyone had told her repeatedly how very fortunate she was.

'Not Dad, was it?' she asked, as her grandmother returned.

'No. David, I assume, is being spoilt to death by Kate Paget, as is usual in your absence.' Mrs Wainwright smiled rather smugly. 'In fact it was young Sam Jefford, and I've asked him round to tea.'

'Then I'd better be off.' Sophie scrambled hastily to her feet.

'Nonsense. Do something to your face and comb your hair while I wash these cups. Or are you going out with Julian this evening?'

Sophie had to admit she was not, and carried the tray into the house, learning that Sam Jefford was an estate agent in Arlesbury. Mrs Wainwright's manner was so elaborately casual, her granddaughter eyed her with suspicion. 'And how come you're pally with an estate agent, Gran?'

'I'll tell you when you come down.'

Sophie knew better than to argue, and ran upstairs to make the necessary repairs, brushing her brown, shoulder-length bob to smoothness and adding a touch of lipstick to the curves of her wide mouth. She eyed her rounded face dispiritedly, contrasting it with Delphine's high cheekbones and slanting gold eyes, remembering with gloom the narrowness of the other girl's hips, her enviable lack of bosom. Sophie had no illusions about her own dimensions, which Mrs Wainwright alluded to firmly as rounded, but Mark and Matthew in rather less complimentary terms.

When Sophie rejoined her grandmother in the garden, that lady wore the look of someone harbouring a gulty secret.

'Is there something you're keeping from me, Gran? Not ill or anything, are you?'

Mrs Wainwright shook her well-groomed head. 'No, dear, I am not ill. I intend selling Greenacre, that's all.'

Sophie stared at her dumbfounded. 'You're giving up this house? Oh Gran—*why*?'

'It's getting too much for me. The garden in particular, now that help is so hard to find these days, and too expensive if one does. I'm not getting any younger, you know.'

Cecily Wainwright was seventy-five, but even in the bright afternoon sunlight looked much less than that, and Sophie told her so, with an emphasis designed to hide her own dismay.

'I've rattled around in this place like a small pea in an oversized pod ever since your grandfather died,' went on Mrs Wainwright, 'and I'm tired of it.'

'Are you buying something smaller?'

'No, darling.' Cecily Wainwright turned a smile of pure mischief on her granddaughter. 'I'm moving into Broad Oaks.'

Sophie's jaw dropped. 'Broad Oaks! But that's a—a——'

'Home for the elderly. I know. I visit my old friend Anne Morton there regularly, and I've had both the time and the opportunity to decide I'll do very well there myself. I can take some of my own furniture if I wish, I'll have a room and bathroom to myself, pleasant communal sitting-rooms if I want company, Anne just along the hall—and I'll take the car, of course. I can go off on trips and have you to lunch just as before, I promise you. But at Broad Oaks I shall have the added bonus of being waited on hand and foot.'

Sophie sat trying to recover from the shock. 'You look far too young for—for Broad Oaks,' she said, after a while. 'Dad will be surprised.'

'David and I are not famous for seeing eye to eye about anything,' said the lady who had been strongly opposed to her daughter's marriage to an impecunious young doctor thirty years earlier. 'But in this case I think he'll agree I'm taking a very sensible step.'

'Why don't you come and live with us?'

'David Gordon and myself under the same roof! Be realistic, child.'

Sophie agreed ruefully that her grandmother was right, then looked up as a car turned in at the gate. 'Is this your estate agent, Gran?'

'Ah, so it is.' Cecily Wainwright smiled with pleasure as a man came across the lawn towards them. He was only a little above medium height and looked rather thin to Sophie, who was used to the burly physique of the Gordon men. Sam Jefford had reddish hair and brown eyes which lit his fine-featured face with charm as he greeted Mrs Wainwright, who introduced him to Sophie, and left the two young people together while she went indoors to make the tea.

Sophie hid a smile, used by now to her grandmother's incessant matchmaking tendencies, and asked the visitor if he lived in Arlesbury.

'I do, indeed. Above the shop now, in fact. I occupy a flat over my premises in Quay Street.'

'Right on the river? How lovely.'

'The place isn't really straight yet. I haven't been in the flat long.'

'You're new to the area, then?' commented Sophie.

He looked embarrassed. 'No, not really. I used to live on the outskirts of the town. Had a house there, but I've just put it on the market.'

'You're in the right line of business for that, then,' said Sophie, hoping to put him more at ease. There was a silent pause, then she got up. 'I'll pop in and help Gran. Shan't be long.' She ran into the house to forestall Mrs Wainwright's effort to heft a loaded tea-tray. 'Hey—give me that. Ladies about to be institutionalised shouldn't go round carrying heavy loads.'

Mrs Wainwright looked cross. 'Why did you leave Sam alone?'

'He seems a bit shy. I thought he'd be better if you came back.'

'He's been going through a bad time, poor boy.'

'Ill?'

'No. Divorced. Acrimoniously, if what I hear is true.'

'The Arlesford jungle drums?'

Mrs Wainwright gave her grandchild a withering look as she shooed her out into the garden, bringing up the rear with the cake-basket used for afternoon tea at Greenacre since time immemorial.

To Sophie's relief Sam Jefford relaxed a little over tea, chatting easily as he praised the moist, crumbly fruitcake and light-as-air scones.

'Wonderful,' he said, as he accepted a second cup of tea. 'Home-made cakes don't feature much in my life.'

'I trust you don't subsist on beans on toast,' said Mrs Wainwright disapprovingly.

'I'm a takeaway man, I'm afraid.' Sam Jefford changed the subject hastily by informing Mrs Wainwright her house would be advertised next day, both in the newspapers and his office windows.

Sophie whistled. 'So soon? Will it take long to sell, do you think?'

He shook his head, smiling. 'Five minutes, at a guess. Perfect decorative order, four bedrooms, idyllic garden and five minutes on foot from the golf-course. Can't lose.'

The talk grew general for half an hour or so, then the visitor got to his feet regretfully. 'Time I was off, I'm afraid. Some homework to do. My secretary's only part-time these days. Pregnant, you know.' He smiled at them. 'You wouldn't happen to know of an efficient secretary on the hunt for a job, I suppose?'

Mrs Wainwright's answering smile was sphinx-like. 'It's just possible I might, Mr Jefford. I'll be in touch with you.'

When she came back to Sophie after seeing the visitor off, Mrs Wainwright sat down with an air of purpose. 'Well?' she demanded. 'Did you like him?'

'He's very nice, Gran.' Sophie grinned. 'Match-making again?'

Her grandmother failed to rise. 'Never mind Sam Jefford. You're the one I'm concerned about, Sophie. I know how much you secretly long to do as all your friends have done, to leave home and gain your independence. Have a place of your own.'

Sophie shrugged. 'Just pie-in-the-sky for me, Gran.'

'Not necessarily.' Mrs Wainwright gazed across the lawn, towards the massed shrubs and trees which marked the boundary of the property. 'I've heard the tenants of Ilex Cottage are moving out shortly, you know. It's very small, and needs doing up, but if you fancy the idea I could arrange for you to have it. Of course, I know Arlesford is no more exciting than Deansbury, but at least it's somewhere different,' she went on. 'Now the boys are off your hands, Sophie, surely David can get a housekeeper and let you lead your own life at last.'

Sophie's eyes glistened at the mere thought. 'Where is the place, Gran?'

'In Church Row.'

Sophie knew the house, the last of a row of what had once been almshouses near the church, in a narrow walk overhung with trees, and very, very private. She came back to earth with a bump. 'Arlesford is thirty miles from Deansbury,' she reminded her grandmother. 'Too far to commute. For me, anyway.'

'Give up your job!'

'I can't, Gran. Especially since Delphine's just walked out on Alexander—I couldn't do the same.'

'Nonsense. Secretaries are no more irreplaceable than brides.' Mrs Wainwright's mouth curved in a very smug smile. 'Use your head, child. I rather fancy you wouldn't have to look far for a job in Arlesford, now, would you? Sam Jefford needs someone very soon, by the sound of it.'

Sophie thought furiously. The idea was tempting. Very tempting indeed. If she could just manage to break her father into the idea gently. Persuade him that her aim was independence rather than desertion. Then she'd be off and running. She shied at the thought of hurting him, but at the same time it was unbearable to think of letting such a golden opportunity slip away.

'You could take whatever you wanted from here to furnish it,' said Mrs Wainwright coaxingly. 'You must make the break some time, child. And, after all, if you decide to marry Julian one day, your father will have to let you go, won't he?'

'Marry Julian?' Sophie shook her head emphatically. 'No chance of that!'

'I just don't understand your generation! If you

feel like that about him, why do you encourage the boy?'

'"The boy" is thirty years old going on fifty, and needs no encouragement, I assure you,' declared Sophie. 'Julian Brett is perfectly happy in his museum, has private means from his mother, and if he wants to spend some of them on entertaining me now and then, who am I to complain? At the very least it means I occasionally eat something I haven't cooked!'

'And I always thought the way to a *man's* heart was via his stomach,' retorted Mrs Wainwright. 'How unromantic you are, Sophie!'

'Yes, I know.' Sophie slid down on her knees and buried her head in her grandmother's lap. 'Bad-mannered, too,' she said with a stifled sob. 'I haven't even thanked you for giving me such a wonderful, wonderful present. And I am going to live in Ilex Cottage, I am, I am—somehow.'

'That's better,' said Mrs Wainwright huskily. 'Now get up. Your tears are ruining my skirt.'

CHAPTER TWO

'CECILY'S going into a home?' Dr Gordon stared incredulously.

'That's right.' Sophie waved him towards the dinner-table. 'Sit down or the food will get cold.'

'It would have been too much to expect her to consult *me* as to her choice, of course,' he said acidly. 'I *am* a doctor. In this one solitary instance I feel I might have been deemed sufficiently knowledgeable to advise her.'

Sophie chuckled. 'How you two do go on. *I* suggested she came to live with us,' she added wickedly, and laughed out loud at her father's expression. 'Don't worry. Her reaction was very similar to yours.'

Dr Gordon was relieved enough to admit that his mother-in-law's choice of domicile was an excellent one, and changed the subject to talk of the Pagets and the débâcle of the wedding that never was, giving it his opinion that Alexander, though undoubtedly better off without someone like Delphine, was nevertheless a great deal more shattered by her desertion than he had allowed anyone to see on that unforgettable day.

'I'm sure he was,' agreed Sophie. 'How Delphine had the nerve to do it I don't know. I'd never have had the bottle.'

'To leave someone waiting at the church—more or less?'

'Exactly. She wouldn't have been the first bride to change her mind, but at least she could have been civilised about it—given Alexander time to cancel everything.'

Dr Gordon's agreement was wholehearted, and they spent the rest of dinner time talking about the twins' return home from their holiday in France, and their almost immediate departure again for Edinburgh.

'It's going to be very quiet without them,' said Dr Gordon pensively, and Sophie's heart sank as she cleared away. It hardly seemed the right time to broach the subject of Ilex Cottage.

Later she brought out a pile of towels and bedlinen waiting for name tapes, and began sewing at a furious rate while her father watched a documentary on television. It had been a wearing day at the office. Perry, who was Alexander's junior partner, had talked incessantly about Delphine's calumny, and by the time Sophie left for the day she was utterly sick of the subject. Fortunately she managed to leave on time and arrived home early enough to make her father's favourite casserole for dinner, with the idea of putting him in a receptive frame of mind for the news that she was contemplating leaving home.

Sophie stitched and snipped, her mind going round and round in the hope of finding a painless way of stating her case. She glanced up at times to find her father equally preoccupied, staring into space rather than at the television, which probably meant Monday at the practice had been hectic, as usual. And every so often Sophie stared into space herself, lost in dreams of the cottage in Arlesford, her eyes lambent with yearning as she imagined herself there, all on her own, with no one to please but herself. She could eat off a tray—a practice much frowned on by Dr Gordon—look at whatever programmes she liked on television. Perhaps not even have a set at all. She sighed heavily. If only there were some way of achieving her object all sublime, without hurting her father in the process.

Sophie snipped off the thread on the last name tape and folded the last bathtowel neatly on top of the pile, aware suddenly that the television was off and her father was staring at her with unaccustomed concentration. She tensed. What now? The look on her father's lined, distinguished face was unsettling.

'Sophie,' he said abruptly, 'have you any thoughts about marrying Julian?'

There seemed to be altogether too much interest in Julian Brett from her loved ones all at once for Sophie's liking.

'Julian's just a friend, Dad,' she said firmly. 'I go out with him mainly because he's not in the least interested in marriage.' To her surprise her father, instead of looking relieved, looked even more troubled. 'Something wrong, Dad?' she asked gently.

Dr Gordon got up, pushed aside the pile of linen and sat down by Sophie on the couch, putting his arm round her and drawing her close.

'Hey!' said Sophie, much alarmed by such unusually demonstrative behaviour. 'What's up, Dad? Something wrong?'

David Gordon drew in a deep breath, plainly

steeling himself to say whatever it was he had to say. 'Sophie, I want you to know how much I appreciate what you've done for us all since—since your mother died. I know you gave up all thoughts of college and career to look after me and the boys——'

'But I never *had* thoughts of college—or a career!'

He brushed this aside. 'Nevertheless I realise what an effort you've made and I want—*we* want to know that your place is with us always, for as long as you want it.'

We? Us? Sophie's eyes were like saucers. 'What *are* you trying to say, Dad?'

'I'm making a right hash of it,' he said wretchedly, 'but I'm trying to break it gently that for some time now, pet, I've been thinking of getting married again. Now I don't want you to feel you're in the way or anything silly like that . . .'

'Married?' breathed Sophie incredulously.

He nodded unhappily. 'But Kate and I agreed——'

'You're going to marry Aunt Kate?' screeched Sophie.

Her father hugged her to him convulsively. 'But it needn't make any difference, I swear. Please don't get upset, sweetheart.'

Sophie pushed him away, beaming all over her face. '*Upset,* you silly old thing! I'm thrilled to bits—I think it's wonderful!' And she gave him a smacking kiss to prove it.

Dr Gordon mopped his face with a handkerchief, letting out a sigh of relief. 'That's why I asked if you intended marrying Julian, Sophie. You've been going out with him for so long, I wondered if you'd put him off because you couldn't leave me.'

'Oh, my beloved father, just wait until I disabuse you of any such ridiculous idea,' said Sophie, almost incoherent with euphoria as she proceeded to tell him all about Ilex Cottage, putting him in the picture at long last as to how much she wanted a little place of her own.

Sophie went round on a pink cloud all her own after hearing her father's news, unaffected even by the miniature mountain of dirty clothes which marked the homecoming of Matt and Mark.

'It's wonderful news,' she told Kate Paget over lunch at the Singing Kettle. 'I can't think why you haven't got together sooner.'

Kate's humorous dark eyes were frank. 'The time wasn't right. Your father wasn't over Louise. Not,' she added quickly, 'that in one way he ever will be, I know.'

Sophie assured Kate that Louise Gordon would have approved strongly. 'Mother liked people to be happy.'

'So do I. Which, I may add, brings me to the subject of your proposed move.' Kate's eyes twinkled. 'People will think your wicked stepmother has turned you out in the snow!'

Sophie giggled, then plunged into news of the cottage, and how she intended to paint and decorate it herself before taking on the job with Sam Jefford. 'Gran made sure the job was mine the moment she heard about you and Dad, of course!'

'Cecily's a born general—but I'm very fond of her. She sent me flowers and a very graceful letter, which I thought was a very nice gesture since I'm marrying her daughter's husband.' Kate sobered. 'Alexander's the one least likely to be overjoyed about your departure, I fancy.'

'Do you think so?' Personally Sophie doubted it. 'I'll work a month's notice *and* train up my replacement. Unlike other ladies I could mention, I have no intention of leaving him in the mire!'

Nevertheless, as the day of Alexander's return grew nearer Sophie's pink cloud gradually evaporated. She saw only too clearly that a man newly returned from a solitary holiday that should have been a honeymoon was unlikely to receive her resignation with joy, if only for the sheer inconvenience of replacing her. The day he was due back Sophie made a special effort with her appearance to boost her morale, and arrived at the office a good half-hour earlier than usual, only to find Alexander had beaten her to it. He was already installed in his office, going through the day's post.

'You're back,' she said idiotically. 'Have you had a good holiday?'

The instant the words left her tongue she regretted them. Idiot! How could he have had a good holiday under the circumstances? A slow tide of colour rose in her face as Alexander looked up at her with one eyebrow raised in the sardonic way she had hated when she was younger.

'Good morning, Sophie. Yes and no.' He smiled very slightly. 'Yes, I'm back, and no, I did not have a good holiday.'

He looked tanned but tired, with dark smudges beneath his eyes. Otherwise he seemed much the same as usual. He stood up to look at some drawings on the frankly antiquarian drawing-board which had served his father and grandfather before him, then shot a look at Sophie, who was hovering unhappily, unsure whether to retreat or stand her ground.

'Go on,' he encouraged. 'Aren't you going to ask me why?'

'No,' she said shortly. 'I have enough sensitivity to realise why, strange as it may seem. I'll come back later if you're not ready to go through the mail. I've got plenty of work left over from yesterday.'

'The others kept you busy, did they?' He sat down behind his desk, clasping his hands behind his head. 'Have they found anyone for the draughtsman's job, by the way?'

'Perry has some candidates lined up for you to see today.'

'Good. Stop fidgeting and sit down, Sophie.'

Sophie did as he said, wondering how soon she could tactfully raise the subject of her resignation. 'How are you, Alexander?' she asked quietly.

'As well as can be expected, I think describes it. I was a fool, of course, to keep to Greece.' His eyes gleamed unseeingly as he stared at her. 'At the time I just needed to run like hell, I suppose, and my bags were packed and the tickets in my pocket, so I kept on going. My mistake was in going alone.' His eyes focused on her suddenly. 'Would you have come, Sophie?'

She suppressed a shudder. 'No fear!'

'Wise girl.' He shrugged his shoulders in the superbly tailored grey jacket. 'Ah, well, it's water under the bridge now. Besides, I hear there's another wedding in the offing.'

Sophie looked at him searchingly. 'Do you mind?'

'Good God, no—I'm delighted. Can't think why the two of them haven't joined forces long since.'

'I must go round in blinkers. The idea never even crossed my mind.'

'And do *you* mind, Sophie?'

Her smile was so incandescent, Alexander blinked. 'Mind? I think it's too marvellous for words.'

He shook his head. 'And there was Kate, afraid you'd feel pushed out into the cold; wicked stepmother syndrome and all that.'

Sophie straightened her shoulders, fixing her dark eyes on him with such intensity, his own narrowed in surprise. 'In actual fact I'm only too delighted to be pushed out. I hadn't intended telling you yet, Alexander. I was going to let you settle in first, but you may as well know now——'

'Don't tell me you're going to marry Julian Brett,' he said sharply.

It was Sophie's turn to blink. 'No. I'm not. I don't know why everyone's in such a hurry to marry me off to Julian these days. We're just friends. Really. He buys me dinner every so often, nothing more.'

'He's been buying you dinner, to my knowledge, for years, Sophie.' Alexander looked at her quizzically. 'It's generally held to be an aisle-job as far as you two are concerned.'

'I have no intention of getting married. To Julian or anyone else.' Sophie's smile was wry. 'Marriage, as I see it, is one long round of cooking, cleaning, shopping—not to mention children who need endless name tapes when they start school.'

'My God—is *that* how you see marriage?'

Alexander eyed her askance. 'You didn't have a word with Delphine on the subject, by any chance? If so, I'm not surprised she walked out on me.'

'I was never on close terms with Delphine.' Sophie looked him in the eye. 'My friends don't indulge in her type of behaviour.'

There was a nasty silence.

'I'm sorry,' she said at last, not really meaning it. 'I suppose I shouldn't have said that.'

Alexander shrugged. 'Please don't apologise. You obviously feel strongly about it. I take it you would not, under the same circumstances, leave it until the last moment to inform your bridegroom you'd changed your mind.'

'Absolutely not. However, since I'm never going to have a bridegroom the occasion is unlikely to arise.' Sophie took in a deep breath. 'But while we're on the subject, Alexander, I consider what Delphine did was barbarous. I know you and I don't always see eye to eye, but believe me, that day my heart bled for you.' She realised her mistake at once. Alexander's expression grew dauntingly forbidding as he turned to the pile of correspondence in front of him.

'How kind, Sophie. Nevertheless, don't waste your sympathy. I'm not likely to pine long. Women are replaceable—even women as beautiful as Delphine. Now, shall we get on, please?'

Smarting from the rebuff, Sophie seethed for the entire hour they spent together on the accumulation of post. She was on her way out of the room when Alexander called her back.

'Weren't you in the middle of telling me something, Sophie?' he reminded her.

'Oh, yes.' Any compunction Sophie had felt beforehand was long gone. 'I'll confirm it in writing, in the usual way, but I thought you should know I'm leaving, Alexander. I'll work the normal month's notice, of course.'

Alexander sat back in his chair, rolling a gold pen between his fingers as he looked at her. 'I feel like a sinking ship,' he murmured after a long, uncomfortable interval.

'I resent the implication, Alexander,' she said tartly. '*I'm* not ratting on you. I'm perfectly willing to find and train up a replacement before I leave.' Her eyes flashed. 'As you remarked not so long ago, women are replaceable. And I, in case you've never noticed it, do happen to be a woman.'

Alexander subjected her to a comprehensive survey, his eyes travelling very slowly from the crown of her shining dark head to the tips of her small black shoes and back again, lingering longest on those curves which reinforced her statement beyond question.

'So you are, Sophie,' he said eventually. 'I'm glad you brought it to my notice.'

Affronted, she turned on her heel and made for the door, but once again he called her back.

'Why, Sophie?'

She turned reluctantly to face him. 'Why what?'

'Why are you leaving me?' His eyes looked unexpectedly bleak. 'I thought this was the ideal set-up for you in your particular situation.'

'Is that why you originally gave me the job?' she demanded.

'No.' Alexander hesitated. 'To be completely honest, I gave you the job because Kate wanted me to.'

'Not because you thought I'd make an efficient secretary,' said Sophie tonelessly.

'No. But I was fortunate. You proved to be a *highly* efficient secretary.'

Sophie stared at him stonily. 'In which case I assume you'll be willing to give me a reference.'

Alexander smiled. 'Since we're soon to be related, won't that smack of nepotism?' He regarded her steadily. 'Besides, I very much want you to stay. If it's a question of more money——'

'Nothing like that,' she said quickly. 'I'm moving out of the district.'

He got up and strolled round the desk. 'Am I allowed to ask where?'

'Of course. Arlesford. Gran's given me a cottage there.'

Alexander bent to pick up a paperclip. 'The one in Church Row?'

'That's right,' said Sophie, surprised. 'You know it?'

'Yes.' He laughed a little. 'I might have known the fair Cecily had a hand in all this. What a lady. If she'd been a few years younger I'd have married *her* instead of making a fool of myself over Delphine.'

Sophie laughed, relieved that Alexander looked less hostile, and told him about her grandmother's bombshell about entering a residential home, and how she'd bulldozed Sam Jefford into giving Sophie a job. 'I'm sure the poor man must have been afraid to say no. He's stuck with me whether he wants me or not.'

Alexander took the pile of letters from her and laid them on the desk, surprising her considerably by taking her hands in his, his eyes very serious as they held hers. 'I've no doubt at all that Jefford wants you, Sophie. He'd be a fool if he didn't, and I know damn well he's no fool. He's too successful for that.'

'You know him, then?' Sophie tried to pull her hands away, but Alexander's long fingers tightened.

'Slightly. Before—before I went away I put him on the track of finding suitable premises for our new branch office.'

'Oh. Small world.' Sophie smiled briskly and pulled out of his grasp. 'I must get on. Perry will be after my services any minute. Do the others know you're back, by the way?'

Alexander nodded. 'I got in touch with both Perry and George Huntley last night.' He handed her the mail. 'Would you do me a very large favour, Sophie?'

She eyed him warily. 'If I can. What is it?'

'Will you come with me for a bar snack at the George at lunch time? To celebrate our parents' nuptials,' he said quickly, as she opened her mouth to refuse. 'And not just that,' he added. 'To be honest I'd very much appreciate a little moral support for my first appearance in public since that God-awful day.'

It was a new experience for Sophie to find Alexander Paget coaxing her for her company. She found she quite liked it. It was rather enjoyable to see the self-sufficient, infinitely superior Alexander waiting rather tensely for her consent.

'Why not?' she said casually.

Gratifying though his answering smile might
have been, thoughts of lunch with Alexander filled
Sophie with foreboding. All morning, even while
she worked with her usual speed and
concentration, she was dogged by the prospect of
running the Deansbury gauntlet in company with
her boss. Normally Alexander's lunches were
working affairs, periods spent making the contacts
vital to the success of a private firm of architects in
a world where competition was fierce and the
biggest plums fell to the most competitive bidders.
Paget & Son were consistently successful in the
Deansbury area, due partly to their long-
established name in the field, partly because the
firm's work was unfailingly excellent, and not least
because of the charisma of Alexander Paget, who
was universally respected as a man of integrity
coupled with a very individual flair. Today,
thought Sophie, sighing, all the world and his wife
would be eager to express their sympathy over
Alexander's recent experience. Hardly a tempting
prospect.

In actual fact the occasion was less trying than
Sophie had expected. The George, a popular place
with business people at lunch time, was thronged
with people pleased to see Alexander in circulation
again. And all of them, to Sophie's surprise,
seemed to take her own presence for granted. Due
to the closeness of their respective families Sophie
and Alexander were often present at the same
family occasions, but Alexander had never actually
taken her out to lunch before, or anywhere else, for
that matter. He was very attentive, she found, also

sensitive to her urge for seclusion, since he seated her in a corner with her back to the room, in a chair which gave her a view of the river outside the windows instead of a sea of curious faces. Sophie chose a glass of white wine and a small salad, refusing Alexander's pleas to try something more exciting.

'No, thanks.' She gave him a cool little smile. 'I rarely eat any lunch at all, except for an apple.'

He frowned. 'Why not?'

'Because I cook what my father calls "a proper dinner" every evening, and if I ate lunch as well I would be even rounder than I am now,' she informed him bluntly, flushing a little as, for the second time that day, Alexander made a leisurely examination of her person, which was clad as usual in garb suited to her job. Sophie made a practice of wearing tailored skirts and shirts to the office, concentrating on quality and cut rather than quantity, and today the skirt was black and straight and the shirt crisp white cotton dotted in black. Her legs were her main vanity, and she invariably wore fine, dark stockings and classic shoes with high heels to compensate for her lack of inches.

'You're not very tall,' said Alexander at last, 'but otherwise I'd have thought you were a very satisfactory size and shape.'

'That's not what you used to say!' said Sophie with feeling, then took a sip of wine, annoyed with herself.

He grinned. 'Well, you *were* rather on the roly-poly side at one time, admit it! But you grew out of that long ago.'

'Only on the outside, Alexander! Inside, due to your relentless teasing when I was at the vulnerable stage, I still feel fat.'

'My God! Is *that* why you treat me with . . .' Alexander thought for a moment. 'Reserve, perhaps?'

'It used to be downright hostility.' She smiled reassuringly. 'But I've mellowed with time.'

'Thank the lord for that.'

At first Sophie found it difficult to enjoy a meal interrupted so often by well-meant expressions of sympathy, but on each occasion Alexander cut short the embarrassed friend by introducing Sophie whether she knew the man or not, and she grew almost used to it after a while, rather surprised when they were eventually left in peace.

'Thank God you came with me, Sophie,' said Alexander, sighing. 'You've been a great help.'

'Perry or George would have done just as well.'

Alexander shook his head, looking more relaxed now the initial ordeal was over. 'Perry was rushing off to meet the latest conquest for lunch, and George went out on that house inspection the other side of Gloucester earlier on. Besides,' he added with a sudden gleam in his eyes, 'neither Perry nor George happens to be a beautiful girl. And a poor, ill-treated male like me needed the company of just such a lady very badly today. Does that sound very chauvinistic?'

'No. Only natural, I suppose. But I'm not beautiful,' said Sophie.

Alexander frowned. 'Who says?'

'My mirror. Not only am I not beautiful, Alexander, I'm neither blind nor equipped with rose-coloured spectacles!'

At that moment yet another sympathiser came to their table to clap a hand on Alexander's shoulder. 'Sincere condolences, old chap,' said the man solemnly, nodding politely to Sophie before he took himself off.

'You'd think I'd suffered a bereavement,' said Alexander savagely.

Sophie regarded him thoughtfully. 'Haven't you?'

He pushed away his half-eaten lunch. 'In a way, I suppose.' He leaned his chin on his hand, looking up at her. 'I suppose the basic truth is that I just never got to know Delphine well enough. She was always flitting about the globe on those modelling assignments of hers, so we spent very little time together if one counts it up in hours. Fate plays some funny tricks, doesn't it, Sophie? If Delphine's family hadn't moved to Deansbury last year I'd never have met her at all.'

'Did she intend carrying on with all the travelling after—afterwards?'

'She insisted she was tired of it. Swore she fancied settling down.' Alexander's smile was crooked. 'I deluded myself she meant it.'

'I could never see what you and Delphine had in common,' said Sophie frankly.

He reached across the table and took her hand. 'To be candid, we had one thing in common which rather overshadowed everything else.'

Sophie coloured and tried to take her hand away. 'No boyish confidences, please, Alexander.'

'Hold on! I was merely trying to explain.' Alexander's grip tightened as he leaned closer. 'For

your ears only, Sophie, to be perfectly truthful I'd
have settled very happily for a less permanent
relationship, but, believe it or not, Delphine held out
for a wedding ring before she'd let me into her bed.'

Sophie stared. 'You mean . . .?'

'That's right, sweetheart. I was allowed to kiss, to
touch as much as I liked, but nothing more. Not until
I'd signed on the dotted line.' Alexander's laugh was
bitter. 'To put it in a nutshell, I'm not only a
laughing stock, but I'm suffering—and I do mean
suffering—from frustration. Plus the knowledge that
I've behaved like several different varieties of fool
over Miss Delphine Wyndham. All of which are new
experiences, I may add.'

Sophie eyed him in consternation, unsure how to
express her sympathy without making things worse.
'I don't think you're a laughing-stock, Alexander,'
she said carefully. 'How could you be? You're a very
popular, respected man in Deansbury. I'm sure no
one has even considered laughing at you.'

His eyes softened. 'Thank you, Sophie.'

She looked away. 'And you're certainly not a fool.
I imagine any man would have done the same for a
girl as beautiful as Delphine.'

'So I'm not a laughing-stock, and I'm not a fool.
That disposes of two of my problems.' Alexander put
a finger under her chin. 'Have you anything to
recommend for the third?'

It slowly dawned on Sophie what Alexander
meant. Right here in the bar of the George he was,
she realised, making some kind of proposition, and,
amazingly, she wasn't as angry as she might have
expected to be, if ever she'd imagined such a situation

arising between them. Not that she would have done in a million years. If their relationship had been slightly more than just employer and secretary from the beginning, it was only because their families had always been friends. Added to which, Alexander had been a such a tower of strength to the boys when their mother died. Sophie regarded him absently as she remembered his patience when the twins, particularly, followed him round like puppies during the time when their father was so shattered. She herself had turned to Kate Paget for comfort, as was only natural, and had never felt as close to Alexander as her brothers did.

'You're very quiet,' he commented, breaking into her thoughts.

'Alexander,' she said tentatively, 'I would have thought this particular problem would have been, well, lessened while you were away.'

'I fully intended it to be.' He smiled crookedly. 'But the other people in the hotel were couples, of varying sorts, and the thought of purchasing a lady's favours—with all the dangers and drawbacks entailed —put a temporary damper on my baser male urges.'

'Were there no other possibilities?' asked Sophie, rather surprised to find she wasn't embarrassed.

'None I cared to pursue.' Alexander released her hand. 'I apologise, Sophie. Forget everything I said.' He looked uncharacteristically contrite. 'I wouldn't blame you if you blacked my eye for even implying you might——'

'Restore your male ego to its former complacency?' Sophie finished for him acidly as she rose to go.

'Not exactly.' He held her jacket for her. 'I think I was just asking for comfort.'

'And I happened to be nearest, I assume.'

'Exactly,' he agreed lightly, and took her by the elbow to steer her through the crowd. 'And possibly dearest, too,' he said in her ear. 'After all, Sophie, you and I are *very* old friends. I was on your particular scene a damn sight earlier than Julian Brett!'

CHAPTER THREE

SOPHIE fully expected to feel awkward with Alexander after their lunch together, but he soon made it plain he felt no regret at having confided in her. In fact, Alexander now behaved towards her as though she were a woman with feelings and opinions to be considered, rather than just little Sophie Gordon who was so efficient and familiar he hardly noticed she was there half the time. These days he was charm itself, and she viewed the charm with suspicion, certain he had an ulterior motive for it. If she hadn't known him better Sophie could have sworn Alexander was pulling out all the stops to make her reconsider her resignation. Not that she had much time for conjecture, since Paget & Son were busier than ever, with the necessity for a new branch growing more urgent by the day.

'I wish your chum Jefford would hurry up and find something in the way of premises,' said Alexander irritably.

'He's not my chum,' Sophie replied.

Alexander smiled in his old, superior manner. 'Better beware, Sophie, when you work for him. He's just divorced his wife, and lonely men are dangerous beasts.' He squeezed her waist unexpectedly as he held the door for her, and Sophie, her arms full of files, was helpless to prevent him.

41

'I say,' said Perry sternly, cannoning into them from the opposite direction, 'would you two mind doing this sort of thing somewhere else, please? There are young, innocent draughtsmen about, you know.'

Alexander's cousin was in his late twenties, with a shock of blond hair a great deal less disciplined than that of his senior partner, and wide blue eyes which gave the lie to the razor-sharpness of the mind behind them.

Sophie included both men in an irritated glare and made for her office, wishing, not for the first time since Alexander's return, that he would revert to his former, pre-wedding-day self, to the time when his attitude towards her had been a lot more impersonal. And a lot easier to put up with, in many ways. She felt on edge most of the time lately, she realised, and put it down to the fact that she was up to her ears at home as well as the office. It was because the twins were leaving home for Edinburgh, she told herself firmly, and applied herself to the task of compiling a short-list from the applications received in response to the advertisement for her own replacement. Alexander flatly refused to have anything to do with it.

'Just weed out three or four from the bunch and I'll see them all on the same day,' he said indifferently. 'Otherwise I don't want to know.'

'But, Alexander, tell me if you want someone young and attractive, or would you prefer mature and reliable——'

'I want *you,* Sophie. But since you're hell-bent on deserting me I don't care a damn who you get in your place, just so long as the woman's literate and can type—and make decent coffee.' Alexander turned from his drawing-board to find Sophie frowning at him in disapproval. 'On reflection,' he added, 'don't get someone too glamorous. George Huntley's blood pressure is suspect and Perry, as you well know, has a very low threshold when it comes to your sex.'

Sophie glared at him. 'I see. You want someone unlikely to disturb you males with her physical charms. Thanks a lot, Alexander. In all the time I've worked here not a soul has ever made the slightest attempt to make a pass at *me*—which should tell me something!'

'My God, I should hope they haven't. They'd have had me to contend with!' He laughed and took her by the shoulders, his eyes teasing. 'Didn't you realise everyone was given the "hands off" instruction right from the word go as far as you're concerned, Sophie, from Perry downwards? I won't include George because he's happily married and wrapped up in his children. The rest know only too well they'd have me to answer to if they started chasing you round your desk.'

Sophie bit her lip. 'Oh. I see.'

'By the way, I almost forgot,' he said casually, 'I took a message for you while you were out to lunch. Brett can't make it tonight. Asked me to apologise for him.'

'Oh, right. Thanks.' Sophie nodded, undismayed.

'Aren't you disappointed?' said Alexander curiously.

'No.' Sophie's dark eyes lit with laughter. 'He was taking me to see some earnest foreign film at the Arts

Centre.'

Alexander shook his fair head in wonder. 'Good God! And you don't mind missing such a treat? How noble, Sophie.'

She chuckled. 'Don't be unkind. Julian's a very nice man, really. It's just that some of his tastes are a little—well, esoteric, that's all.'

Alexander's eyes glinted. 'Esoteric? What *do* you both get up to, may I ask?'

'Don't be disgusting!' she snapped.

He wagged a reproving finger. 'Now, now, Sophie. All I meant was poetry-reading, board-games and so on. Nothing naughty.'

Sophie flushed bright red and dived for the door, but Alexander caught her before she reached it and held her lightly.

'Sophie,' he said softly, 'let me take you out to dinner tonight, instead.'

In the time it took for Sophie's colour to subside her mind worked at a furious rate. She was highly suspicious of this new Alexander, the one who'd taken to teasing her and touching her and generally making it impossible to ignore that lately his attitude towards her had taken a decided U-turn. He was missing Delphine, she reminded herself, and behaving in the main with exemplary stoicism about it. Nevertheless, Sophie couldn't rid herself of a nagging suspicion which grew stronger by the day. Preposterous though it might seem, she was beginning to believe Alexander had elected to seek balm for his wounds from the last source she would ever have expected. Her own.

'Well?' he prompted. 'Will you, Sophie?'

'I can't,' she said. 'I'm cooking dinner for Dad and the boys as usual. I wasn't meeting Julian until later on.'

Alexander released her and stood back, still regarding her in the same unsettling fashion. 'Just a thought. Some other time, perhaps, before you finally shake the dust of Deansbury from your shoes.'

'Yes. Lovely.' Sophie smiled brightly and retreated to her office, which was small and cramped, but blessedly private, with a door she could shut on the rest of the workforce at Paget & Sons.

'Kate's coming round after dinner,' announced Dr Gordon, as the family gathered round the table later that evening. 'Thought we'd thrash out a few plans for the wedding.'

Matthew Gordon, large and dark like his father, received his plate with interest. 'What's this?'

'Beef olives.'

Mark, who was a carbon copy of his brother, gave a loud whistle. 'Touch of the *haute cuisine,* no less. Special occasion?'

'No. I got home early for once, and thought I'd try something different.' Sophie tasted her own portion cautiously. 'Hm. The garlic's a bit violent.'

'It's very good,' her father assured her, then grinned. 'Cast-iron defence against vampires, too.'

Sophie apologised, laughing, but the twins were enthusiastic. Their sojourn in France had given them a taste for the exotic and they ate heartily. Not, in their sister's opinion, that they ever did anything else.

'All our name tapes on?' asked Matt.

'Of course, O Master. Everything's ready for the off. And if you unpack anything else and wear it I'll throttle you,' warned Sophie.

Dr Gordon scrutinised his daughter's tired face. 'Busy day today, love?'

'Very. On top of the usual stuff, I'm trying to find someone to replace me. Not many of the applications are very promising so far.' Sophie felt dispirited, wondering now why she'd been ambitious enough to cook such a complicated meal at the same time as finishing off the twins' ironing.

'How's Alexander?' asked Mark. 'Pining for the tasty Delphine?'

'How would I know?' said Sophie shortly.

'Alexander's not the type to show his feelings to the world at large,' observed her father. 'Though Kate is amazed at how well he's taken it.' He fixed his sons with a peremptory eye. 'You two, by the way, can do the washing up. Sophie's going out with Julian.'

Sophie disabused him of this idea, and braced herself for the usual barrage of teasing over Julian, who'd never managed to win her brothers' approval. Ignoring them with the ease of long practice, she went to sit with her father, leaving the pots and pans to the noisy ministrations of the twins while she curled up in a corner of the sofa to watch the news. She thought half-heartedly about tidying herself, but decided against it, thinking Aunt Kate was unlikely to mind a shiny nose and faded old denims just for once.

'Something worrying you, pet?' asked Dr Gordon.

Sophie smiled absently, her eyes on the screen.

'No, Dad. I'm fine.' She turned to look at him. 'I'm off to look at the cottage on Saturday, by the way, and since it's my Sunday at Gran's and the twins will have gone by then, I thought I'd stay the night at Greenacre.'

'Of course, pet.' He looked up as the doorbell rang. 'Kate, I expect.'

'I'll go,' yelled Matt from the kitchen, and to Sophie's consternation could be heard exclaiming in delight as a familiar voice greeted him at the door.

Alexander, it seemed, had decided to accompany his stepmother.

Kate came into the room to be kissed by David Gordon, her eyes apologetic as she gave Sophie a hug. 'I know you've been stuck with my son all day, too, love, but Alexander volunteered to drive me over. It's a bit foggy tonight.'

Alexander sauntered into the room, smiling, looking rather different from the sober-suited architect of the day in a yellow polo shirt and khaki cord trousers, Mark and Matthew hot on his heels as usual. He greeted Dr Gordon and Sophie with the air of a man confident of his welcome.

As he had a right to be, conceded Sophie, trying to be fair. They were all fond of Alexander, she told herself firmly, her brothers more than herself, of course. Indeed, Mark and Matthew seized on him at once, talking their heads off in unison about their eagerness to be off to Edinburgh, and Sophie retreated into her sofa-corner while her father poured drinks.

'You won't know what to do with yourself with those two off your hands, Sophie,' said Kate, joining

Sophie.

'Bliss,' agreed Sophie. 'How those boys eat! I'm sure Tim never ate so much when he was their age. Dad told you Tim wrote to say how pleased he was about the wedding?'

Kate nodded, her eyes warm. 'You've all been so good about it.'

'And why wouldn't we be?' Sophie smiled wickedly. 'I'm not losing a father, after all—only gaining a very lovely stepmother. Plus another brother to add to my tally,' she added deliberately.

Alexander looked up sharply. 'What was that?'

When Kate repeated Sophie's comment, he looked unamused. 'While I,' he said drily, 'seem to be losing out all round—first a bride, now a secretary.'

Sophie hugged her drawn-up knees, wishing she were somewhere else, but Matt bridged the awkward little silence with his usual blithe disregard for sensitivity.

'We were thrown by the news, Alexander. Who'd have thought Delphine would play a dirty trick like that? Pretty foul, if you ask me.'

'But no one has, Matthew,' said his father, 'so let us forget about the incident in question—my apologies, Alexander—and talk about Kate and me instead.'

Alexander held up his hand promptly. 'Could I, as son and giver-away of the bride, make one request, David?'

Dr Gordon nodded good-humouredly.

'Do you intend marrying in church?' Alexander's flexible mouth turned down at the corners. 'I know it's not up to me, of course, but I'm sure I speak for

Kate as well as myself when I say I don't think I could face another session in Deansbury Register Office!'

There was sympathetic laughter as David Gordon assured him the wedding would certainly be quiet, with only immediate family and one or two friends, but quite definitely in church.

'Aunt Kate,' said Sophie a little later, while the men were engaged in a discussion, 'are you inviting Gran?'

'Of course, love.' Kate looked surprised. 'Why? Do you think she won't want to come?'

'No, no. I'm sure she'll be delighted. I thought maybe you wouldn't care for the idea.'

Kate patted her hand. 'I wouldn't exclude her for the world. You can tell her this weekend that an official invite will arrive as soon as I get them printed.'

'What are you two whispering about?' Alexander joined them, making Kate move up so he could wedge himself between her and Sophie. 'Girlish confidences?'

'No. We were talking about Gran.' Sophie retreated as far as she could, but Alexander promptly moved with her, so that she was trapped.

'Ah, the divine Cecily,' he said, putting an arm along the back of the sofa. 'Hers was just one of several calls I had this evening after you went, Sophie.'

Sophie frowned at him in surprise. 'Gran phoned you? Business or pleasure?'

'A little of each. She asked me if I'd do a house inspection on the cottage in Arlesford before you move in, and of course I agreed. I wouldn't dare do otherwise!' He laughed into Sophie's surprised eyes, and moved his arm to hold her shoulders lightly. 'She said you were going to see the place on Saturday and suggested I go with you to look over it for dry rot or rising damp. So the survey is business, your company the pleasure.'

Sophie shifted restlessly, aware that the twins were taking great interest in the location of Alexander's arm. 'Are you sure Saturday's convenient? It seems a bit unfair to encroach on your weekend.'

'Not at all. There's nothing I'd rather do.'

'I'm relieved, Alexander,' said Dr Gordon. 'Since Sophie's set her her heart on living in that poky little cottage, I'd be glad to know the place is fit for human habitation.'

The telephone rang and Mark rushed off to answer it, returning to say Julian was on the line for Sophie. She scrambled thankfully from her corner, glad to escape. After listening patiently to a few minutes of Julian's apologies and suggestions for another evening out, she got back to find the twins had gone off to the local to meet friends, and in their absence Alexander had offered the bridal pair the Chantry, which was the house left to him by his father, and which he currently shared with Kate.

Sophie looked at him in surprise, well aware that he had intended living there with Delphine. Kate's original plan had been to move in with a widowed sister when Alexander married, but under the circumstances she had stayed on at the Chantry.

Alexander smiled. 'It's rather a spur-of-the-moment decision, but I've been given the option on a house I've had my eye on for some time, so I thought David could take over the Chantry with Kate.'

Kate took Sophie's hand in hers. 'David and I have been mulling over where to live ever since we decided to join forces. Even though none of you will be living with us permanently, I'd still like a house where there was a room you could each call your own. Tim included, when he gets tired of his Aussie sheep. Alexander's solution seems perfect.'

Dr Gordon nodded with enthusiasm. 'I'll put this one on the market immediately, then between us Kate and I should see Alexander's not out of pocket on the deal.'

Sophie looked at Alexander curiously. 'Where is the house you have in mind?'

'Oh, didn't I tell you?' he said casually. 'Your future boss has been very busy on my behalf. He's secured a house in Brading for me, and at the same time found the exact office premises I've been after for the firm.'

Sophie felt distinctly nettled. It was the first she'd heard of it. 'How fortunate. Are the premises large?'

'Slightly smaller than the Deansbury offices, but more than adequate.'

'Whereabouts in Brading?' asked Dr Gordon with interest.

'The house is at the end of Cheynies Lane. I did the original plans for it years ago when my father was alive. River frontage, very private, just what I want.' Alexander paused, smiling, while Kate looked down with sudden interest at a loose thread on her sleeve. 'But the office premises aren't in Brading after all, Sophie. Sam Jefford snapped some up in Sheep

Street in Arlesford.'

'Arlesford!' Sophie looked from Alexander's bland smile to Kate's uneasy face. 'Did *you* know about this, Aunt Kate?'

'Not until tonight.'

Sam Jefford, Alexander informed them, had rung just before he left the office. Some office premises had just come into his hands, and since they were right in the commercial centre of Arlesford he advised snapping them up immediately.

'And the house in Brading?' asked Sophie coolly. 'Did that come on the market today, too?'

'Er—no, not exactly. I went to see Jefford some time ago, actually. I'd been given the nod that Willow Reach might soon be up for sale.' Alexander smiled warily. 'I thought I'd kill two birds with one stone, vet your future employer at the same time—make sure he was a suitable type for you to work for.'

Sophie was so incensed at this, she never even noticed when her father led Kate from the room. She sprang up, eyes flashing, infuriated by the thought that her new life in Arlesford looked like being less free of the old one than she'd imagined.

'How very busy you've been, Alexander—downright interfering, in fact!' She battled to keep back tears of sheer temper. 'Why does everybody think I'm incapable of running my own life?' She dashed a hand across her eyes impatiently. 'Gran heard of the cottage—which is wonderful, I know, but then even *she* couldn't leave me to find my own job. She even organises you to go over the cottage with me. While you, Alexander Paget, have the sheer cheek to take it on yourself to check up on Sam Jefford's pedigree, not to mention the amazing coincidence of his finding premises for you in the very town where I intend to live. There were other premises, Alexander. I write your letters, remember. Perry's too. You could have had a place in Gloucester——'

'Too much competition.'

'Or Bristol——'

'Too expensive.'

Sophie's eyes flashed dangerously. 'I see. It just had to be Arlesford.'

'It was, I swear, sheer coincidence, Sophie.' Alexander moved nearer, but she backed away, her eyes dangerously bright.

'Even Dad seems to have some crazy idea of marrying me off to Julian Brett!' She paused, sniffing angrily. 'Perhaps it's not such a crazy idea. Julian, at least, doesn't try to run my life for me.'

Alexander's face darkened. 'None of us is trying to run your life, Sophie. We just want to take care of you, that's all—keep a friendly eye on you.'

'Oh, yes? And if all had gone to plan, and you were now living happily ever after with Delphine, would you, personally, still be so damn eager to keep an eye on me? Doesn't all this sudden rush of feeling stem from the fact that you've been thrown over by one woman and I just happen to be on hand as convenient target practice for that wounded ego of yours?'

Alexander had been standing with his hands in his pockets, but at her last words he removed them quickly and grabbed her by the shoulders, pushing her over to the mirror to stand close behind her so that she could see their reflections together; Alexander, his thick fair hair lying close to the classical shape of his head, his eyes glittering like a tiger's between his thick, dark lashes. And there's me, thought Sophie dismally. Hair like a bird's nest, eyes swollen, nose red, and tastefully attired in one of the twins' shrunken sweatshirts.

'If,' said Alexander, in a chillingly soft voice, 'transient physical comfort was my sole aim, Sophie Gordon, don't you think I might have chosen a lady just a trifle more suitable—from a purely male standpoint?'

The words acted on her like a cold wind, drying her tears like magic. She shrugged free of his hands. 'How stupid of me. You're right, of course. I'm a complete idiot.'

Alexander moved towards her, but Sophie flinched away.

'Don't——' she said sharply, and Alexander stepped back, his face set in grim lines.

'You mistook my meaning,' he said urgently, then cursed under his breath as Kate came in with Dr Gordon.

'Finished fighting, you two?' she said gaily. 'I've made some tea.'

With enormous effort Sophie managed to smile, aware all at once that her head was pounding. 'I wonder if you'd all excuse me? I don't feel very marvellous—must have been the garlic.' She swallowed hard, gave a stifled moan and fled upstairs to part violently with her dinner, then stripped her clothes from her shivering body and crawled into bed, like a small animal burrowing into its nest for shelter.

CHAPTER FOUR

SHEER willpower forced Sophie out of bed next morning to face her father over the breakfast-table.

'You look like something the cat dragged in,' said Dr Gordon, and took her pulse. 'Let me see your tongue.'

Sophie stuck it out obediently and Dr Gordon took one look, told her to put it away and gave her back her hand.

'Let me ring Alexander and tell him you're not up to going in today.'

Sophie yearned to succumb to such temptation, but somehow held firm. 'No, Dad. Too much on. Anyway, it was only the beef olives.' She shuddered. 'Never again.'

Dr Gordon looked sceptical. 'The rest of us managed to survive them unscathed. Kate was very worried about you. She popped up to take a look at you before I drove her home, but she said you were asleep.'

Sophie had been lying low, not asleep, but instead of saying so seized on an interesting point. 'Why did *you* drive her home?'

'Alexander left once you went off to bed. Said he had some work to do, so I asked Kate to stay on for a while.' He smiled at his wan daughter. 'Must have been quite an argument you two had, since you rushed off to throw up and Alexander rushed off to his drawing-board. Just like the old times, in fact, when you two argued about everything. I thought you were both past that stage long since.'

'Alexander seems to imagine he has some right to interfere in my life.' Sophie drained her teacup thirstily. 'Sees his role as Big Brother, not stepbrother.'

'When you were together on the sofa last night I received the distinct impression that Alexander didn't see himself in the light of your brother at all.' Dr Gordon got up, patting her head before collecting his medical bag. 'And don't flash those eyes at me, pet. I'm only a poor benighted father trying to bring up his daughter the best way he can.'

Sophie grinned at such blatant bathos. 'Oh, go and minister to someone else. I'm fine. Or I shall be after I've drunk a gallon of tea.'

Rather to her own surprise, Sophie was right. By the time she'd drunk the teapot dry she felt sufficiently restored to do battle with her appearance, and achieved a creditable result with extra blusher and eyeshadow, plus the morale-lift of a new cream silk shirt striped in black, with a black satin bow tied under the cream collar. Worn with her usual trim, black skirt and slender-heeled shoes the effect was both efficient and pleasing. Nothing, however, helped with the sinking feeling in her stomach at the prospect of facing Alexander. Sophie felt neither of them had emerged from the previous night's encounter with honours, and wished fervently she could leave her job at once, instead of keeping to her promise to train her own replacement.

By the time she reached the premises of Paget & Son in the market square Sophie had worked herself into an unprecedented state of nerves, only to find that Alexander was not, as was his custom, at his desk before she arrived. Perry called from his own sanctum instead, which was unusual. Punctuality in the mornings was not one of Perry's strong points.

'Alexander told me to remind you he's in court all day today,' he announced, his face concerned as he looked at her more closely. 'I say, Sophie, you feeling rough, love?'

'Stomach bug,' said Sophie briefly, privately delirious with joy that Alexander had elected to go straight to court instead of coming first to the office as he usually did. She felt better at once, and settled herself thankfully to work through the day's mail with Perry instead. Lunch was a cup of tea taken alone in her office, while she just sat doing nothing at all until her lunch hour was over, much of the time spent in resisting the urge to type her notice, leave it on Alexander's desk and never darken his door again. Which was a pretty impractical move, Sophie reminded herself, since they would soon be linked, however loosely, by the marriage of their respective parents. She worked with a will during the afternoon, comforted by the prospect of a morning off next day to help get the twins away on their journey to Edinburgh. She was grateful for any breathing space she could get before confronting Alexander again, and went cold all over every time she thought of the way Alexander had made it so crystal-clear that any amatory intentions on his part had been the product of her own imagination.

When she arrived home Sophie was relieved, and touched, to find that the twins had organised their own farewell dinner, in the shape of many and varied dishes from the local Indian takeaway, neither of the boys backward in disposing of their queasy sister's share of the spoils. When they'd taken themselves off for a final carouse down at the local pub, Sophie took her father's advice and went early to bed after a supper of toast and tea, and woke next day in better shape to cope with the frantic last-minute chaos as her excited brothers packed their old transit van ready to set off for the delights of Freshers' Week at Edinburgh University. Sophie felt a sharp pang as the battered van finally rolled away down the drive, taking her young brothers on the first leg of adulthood. She was glad of her father's arm around her as they turned back into the house.

'We'll miss them,' said Dr Gordon gruffly, and Sophie smiled, determinedly cheerful.

'But far fewer shirts and plates to wash!'

When Sophie arrived at the office after lunch Alexander was there right enough, but too pre-occupied to pay attention to his secretary. Builders were in and out of the office all afternoon as he worked through a list of them, systematically vetting which of them were most suitable to tender for construction of a large superstore on the outskirts of the town.

Since Alexander was fully occupied, Sophie took the opportunity of writing to the four most promising aspirants for her own job, requesting the chosen ladies to attend for interview the following week. She was obliged to interrupt Alexander once to collect his diary to make sure which day was best, but he barely acknowledged her discreet murmur of apology, and Sophie withdrew quickly, more than content to keep as low a profile as possible. When it was time for her to leave Alexander was still tied up with the last of the builders, and she waited a while, reluctant to interrupt him again. Eventually, even though it was Friday evening, she decided to take the unusual course of going off without informing Alexander, said goodnight to Perry and left for the weekend with a sigh of relief.

Sophie woke with a start the following morning to repeated rings of the doorbell. She peered at her clock, bleary-eyed, to find it was eight-thirty, which meant her father would already have left for his Saturday-morning surgery. Yawning, she dragged a dressing-gown over her pyjamas and went down-stairs, expecting to confront the postman. Her jaw dropped when she opened the door to find Alexander smiling at her as he jogged energetically on the spot. He looked depressingly fit and fresh in a black tracksuit and running shoes, his hair only a very little ruffled by his daily morning run.

'Morning, Sophie. Thought I'd check what time you want to start for Arlesford,' he said cheerfully.

Sophie felt murderous. She dragged her dressing-gown closer round herself, horribly conscious of the spectacle she presented. 'I'm going on my own,' she said acidly.

'Don't be silly. Cecily told me to escort you, so escort you I shall.' He smiled kindly, as though she were a fractious child. 'Not still peeved with me, are you, Sophie? Run along, there's a good girl. I'll be back for you in an hour.'

Before Sophie could voice her objections Alexander was off, making for home at a pace that tired Sophie to watch. Irritably she banged the door shut and went upstairs to shower, fulminating, not for the first time recently, over her beloved grandmother's autocratic ways, and convinced the last thing in the world Alexander really wanted to do was potter about in a chilly old cottage on a Saturday.

Nevertheless, Sophie was ready and waiting when Alexander's Mercedes roadster slid to a stop outside the gate exactly an hour later. By this time she felt more composed, largely due to the fact that her hair was shining, her face made up with great care to look as nature intended it to look, and she was wearing her favourite brown cords and cream wool shirt, with an apricot mohair sweater knotted loosely over her shoulders by its sleeves. Not of a mind to let Alexander think she was over-eager, she deliberately hid in her bedroom and let him ring the doorbell twice before going downstairs to let him in. Her greeting was coolly polite as she asked him if he'd care for coffee before they set off.

Alexander, dressed in ancient denims which clung lovingly to his long legs, wore a shirt rather similar to Sophie's, with a fleece-lined denim jacket slung over his shoulders. He assented with enthusiasm, settling himself on a high stool in the kitchen while she made instant coffee in yellow pottery mugs.

'I'm sorry about the other night, Sophie,' he said, taking the wind out of her sails. 'I think you totally misunderstood what I said.'

'I don't remember what you said,' lied Sophie

without turning a hair. 'I just wasn't feeling well. My dinner disagreed with me.'

'I was afraid the news about the new premises was the real culprit.' His smile was disarming. 'I promise you, Sophie, it was sheer coincidence that Sam Jefford happened to find the ideal place in Arlesford. I'm not trying to breathe down your neck, scout's honour. Not that the idea lacks appeal,' he added very deliberately.

Sophie scowled at him over her coffee. 'I wish you wouldn't say things like that, Alexander. You never used to. I preferred it when you treated me like part of the furniture.'

'Did I?' Alexander shook his head disapprovingly. 'No wonder you don't want to work for me any more!'

'You know that isn't the reason,' she said, exasperated. 'I just want a change. It's nothing personal.'

'Then if it's nothing personal, my little friend, what objection do you have to seeing something of me socially?' Alexander's handsome face wore an expression of such friendly reason, Sophie thawed a little.

'Well, none, I suppose,' she said with caution. 'If that's all you have in mind, fine.'

'Good.' He slid off the stool, and took her by the hand. 'Come on, then, let's go.'

The air held a tang of autumn, the leaves on the trees just beginning to turn along the sunlit minor roads Alexander chose in preference to the swift, busy bypass which linked Arlesford to Deansbury. Sophie relaxed in the luxurious car, not at all averse

to a journey enjoyed in such comfort rather than in
the bus she would have caught otherwise. And any
traces of constraint she felt were soon dispelled by
Alexander's matter-of-fact attitude as he weighed up
the merits of the four applicants Sophie had lined up
for the following week, then went on to discuss the
possibility of winning the job of designing a large,
luxury hotel on the river at Brading.

'Are you likely to get it, do you think?' asked
Sophie. 'The competition's bound to be fierce.'

Alexander was optimistic. By a stroke of luck he
had obtained outline planning permission for the
owner of the land in the first place, which gave him
an edge when the owner sold the land to the hotel
chain. 'Fancy taking a look at the spot?' he asked.
'We'll still have plenty of time to look over the
cottage this afternoon.'

Sophie agreed readily. Brading was a picturesque
place, hardly more than a large village on the banks
of the Avon, and very popular with people who
commuted from it daily to Bristol and Bath and even
as far as London. The site for the hotel was a prime
spot, with riparian rights along a sizeable stretch of
river. Alexander parked the car near a group of
willows overlooking a view of trees and sunlit, slow-
moving water, and cattle grazing on the
watermeadows on the far side of the river.

'The hotel aims to be one of those places you can
get away from it all for a restorative type of weekend
break. Indoor heated pool, jacuzzis, gymnasium,
landscaped grounds with tennis courts, as many of
the original trees as possible.' Alexander's eyes
gleamed as if he could see it all taking shape on his

drawing-board.

'Sounds idyllic.' Sophie hesitated, then curiosity got the better of her. 'Is the house you're buying near here?'

Alexander nodded. 'Would you like to see it?' His eyes were indulgent as he smiled at her, and Sophie's answering smile was wry. 'What is it?' he asked quickly.

'I was just thinking how kind and brotherly you are today!'

'Yes,' he agreed smugly. 'I am, aren't I?'

Sophie laughed as he drove off, looking about her with interest as the car turned off on an unadopted road which led along the riverbank for a mile or so without sight of another house until it ended in high laurel hedges and tall wooden gates.

'This is Willow Reach,' said Alexander in a proprietorial tone. He helped Sophie out of the car then twisted the iron ring that served as handle and swung open one of the metal-studded gates for her to go through into a garden she gazed at in wide-eyed delight. The smooth green lawns and herbaceous borders were conventional enough, but her attention was caught immediately by an avenue of yews cut in fantastic shapes, thrones, flowers, birds and beasts of every description drawing the eye towards a grotto where beckoning stone nymphs balanced stone conch-shells above a marble-rimmed pool.

'The fountain needs repair, I'm afraid,' said Alexander. 'What do you think of my new home?'

Sophie tore her eyes away from the grotto and turned to the house, which was built of age-mellowed stone to a design which was strangely timeless.

Countless small panes of glass had been used to make up the windows which dominated the mellow rose-gold walls, and a wistaria-hung veranda ran along the lower half of the house to form a balcony for the upper rooms.

'This,' said Alexander softly, 'was the first house I ever designed, long before you came to work with me, Sophie.'

'It's quite lovely, but——' Puzzled, Sophie turned from the house to the garden, then back again. 'If you designed it the house must be new, of course, yet it doesn't *look* modern, and I just can't believe that the atmosphere in this garden was achieved in a few short years.'

'Clever girl,' he said with approval. 'The original house was left empty for years, then the owner died, and this part of his estate was sold by the heir. My father acquired it, knocked down some of the house, which was much bigger than this, but kept all the building material worth saving and gave me the job of not only designing a house to rise, phoenix-like, from the ruins of the old one, but to ensure it blended happily with the existing garden, once it had been cleared. When Father first brought me here I quite expected to find a princess fast asleep somewhere in the middle of it!'

Sophie wandered round the house, peering through the windows at empty light-filled rooms with gleaming wood floors. 'Do you have a key, Alexander? Can we go in?'

'Afraid not. I haven't actually signed the contract yet.'

They spent a peaceful hour exploring the delights

of the walled garden on the other side of the grotto, where apples and pears ripened on espaliered trees and the autumn sun was warm. Afterwards they strolled down to the small, private jetty, where a dilapidated rowing-boat moved languidly to and fro at its mooring. They sat on an old stone bench near a line of willows at the water's edge, and Alexander explained how luck had been with him the night he'd been invited to a dinner given as a farewell party for the couple who lived in the house.

'They had actually sold it, packed up and moved out, and were almost on the point of leaving for Australia to join their children, when the sale fell through.'

'So you jumped in.'

'I couldn't resist the opportunity. I got on to Sam Jefford with the speed of light, believe me, when they told me he was handling the re-sale.'

'When will you move in?'

'As soon as I can. I need basics like curtains and some carpets, and in any case I thought I'd wait until Kate and David's wedding before I move out of the Chantry.'

Sophie was very thoughtful as they went back to the car, surprised to find herself almost unwilling to leave the tranquillity of the hidden, dreaming garden. 'It's so beautiful here,' she said, as Alexander swung the heavy gate shut and twisted the great iron ring to secure it.

'Too quiet for some,' said Alexander.

'Delphine, you mean?'

'Can you imagine her tucked away from the world here?' His tone was derisory. 'She was unenthusiastic

about living in this part of the world at all. She did
her best to persuade me to set up practice in London,
even go to work for one of the big international
firms. Willow Reach was never meant for someone
like Delphine.'

Sophie was in total agreement, unable to picture
the very contemporary Delphine in that sleeping,
secluded garden, glad the gold, predatory eyes had
never looked in disparagement on the house that was
Alexander's brainchild.

As they set off again Alexander suggested they
lunch at an inn on the outskirts of Arlesford to give
them energy for the task ahead.

'Energy?' said Sophie with suspicion. 'What am *I*
expected to do?'

'Hold the other end of a tape, if nothing else.'
Alexander ushered her into the comfortable restaurant bar of the Feathers, where a fire was burning in
the large cowled fireplace, regardless of the sunshine
outside. They ordered home-made meat and potato
pies, free of garnish of any kind other than great
crusty rolls and fresh farmhouse butter.

'No use asking for chilli con carne or pasta here,'
said Alexander, as they began on their meal with
appetite. 'The lady of the house makes everything
herself, and believes in plain, homespun fare cooked
with loving care.'

'Amen,' said Sophie reverently, mouth full. 'This
is the first square meal I've eaten since those horrible
beef olives.'

'Which made you so crotchety, I suggest you never
cook them again.' Alexander grinned at her across
his tankard of beer.

'You were the one who made me angry, telling me I looked too much of a fright to attract any man,' she countered, throwing down the gauntlet.

'Is *that* what you thought I meant?' he said blankly. 'Good God! Slight communication problem, I assure you, Sophie. I meant something very different.'

'Whatever it was, I don't want to know,' she said flatly. 'Let's keep things friendly. Draw a veil over Wednesday.'

Alexander seemed on the point of saying something, then shrugged and went on with his lunch, following Sophie's lead when she introduced more neutral topics. After a pleasant hour or so they went on into Arlesford where Alexander parked his car in a small car park near the river, not eager to risk leaving his beloved Mercedes outside Ilex Cottage, where only a narrow walk separated the houses from the churchyard.

'Cecily says the people next door have the spare key, which saves us driving out to Greenacre first,' said Alexander, as they walked up the steepish hill towards the church. 'You'll be able to meet your new neighbours.'

Sophie preferred to do this on her own, and insisted Alexander wait some distance away while she knocked on the door of the adjoining cottage. The elderly lady who handed over the key was friendly and very jolly, also unashamedly curious about the tall, fair man waiting along the lane.

'That your husband, dear?' she asked hopefully.

Sophie denied it firmly. 'No. Mr Paget's come with me to do a survey on the house,' she said, loud

enough for Alexander to hear clearly, since Mrs
Perkins admitted to being a little hard of hearing.

'You might have introduced me,' objected
Alexander, as he unlocked the door of Ilex Cottage.
'Even if I can't count myself honoured enough to be
your husband.'

'No point. You're hardly likely to meet Mrs
Perkins again.'

The look Sophie received was quizzical as
Alexander ushered her into the sitting-room, which
looked bigger than anticipated.

'Because it's empty, I suppose,' said Sophie,
delighted, and ran through into the tiny kitchen,
which was fitted with a very up-to-date oven and
refrigerator, to her surprise. After a rapid inspection
of the neat little cupboards Sophie made for the stairs
which led from a door in the sitting-room to a tiny
landing between a cupboard of a bathroom and the
solitary bedroom, which boasted a bow-window like
the room below.

Alexander followed her up with more care, obliged
to duck his tall head before entering the bedroom. He
winced at the sight of the wallpaper which was,
Sophie had to admit, somewhat arresting, with a
design of roses and looping ribbon bows, and quite
overpowered the proportions of the room. Alexander
removed strips of paper in strategic areas to look for
damp, but found nothing to cause concern. Then he
swung himself up into the loft space and spent some
time inspecting the roof from the inside with a
powerful torch, while Sophie went back downstairs
to indulge in much mental interior decoration. By the
time Alexander joined her she had dispensed with the

patterned wallpaper, painted the walls white, hung yellow and white chintz at the windows and set flowering plants in the deep window embrasure.

'Isn't it perfect?' she said blissfully, as Alexander ducked into the room, brushing cobwebs from his hair.

'I'm not certain about perfect, but as far as I can see the roof's all right and there's no sign of dry rot. You've got a bit of woodworm, of course—inevitable in a house of this age—but nothing that can't be treated.'

'So it's all right?' she pressed. 'Nothing to stop me moving in?'

'I'll see,' he said non-committally, and it was another two hours before he passed final judgement, confirming that the basic structure was sound, there was no sign of settlement anywhere, the drainage system was satisfactory, and only a few tiles on the roof would need to be replaced.

Sophie flung her arms round Alexander and kissed his cheek in euphoria. He laughed, returning the embrace with interest.

'If that's my reward for a survey, what would I get for a helping hand with the decorating?'

CHAPTER FIVE

SOPHIE leaned back against his joined hands, her eyes frankly calculating. '*You,* Alexander? Can you really paint and so on?'

'I'd have you know I'm the Picasso of the home-decorating world,' he said solemnly. 'And, as regards the "so on", I'm unequalled!'

'No, seriously! *Would* you help me do the place up?'

'I take it you're willing to put up with my company so long as I make myself useful!'

'That's right.' Sophie pulled free, laughing. 'Perry, too, if he can paint.'

'I claim sole rights or none at all,' said Alexander promptly. 'Including Julian Brett,' he added.

'Julian wouldn't know one end of a paintbrush from the other.' She eyed him uncertainly. 'Do you mean it?'

'I do.' He strolled over to the door to examine the lock. 'But I'd want something in return, of course.'

'Oh, yes?'

'Help me choose curtains and carpets for Willow Reach.' He looked up, grinning at the surprise on her face. 'I'm making Kate a present of the stuff at the Chantry, naturally. Besides, Willow Reach has a very definite personality all its own. I want to please it with my choice.'

Sophie smiled. 'You talk as though the house were a person.'

'Since I designed it, I'm entitled to my feeling of affinity, Sophie.' Alexander glanced at his watch. 'Time we were off. I'd better deliver you to your grandmother at the gallop. I'm due back in Deansbury by seven.'

Cecily Wainwright ignored Alexander's refusal of tea. 'Nonsense,' she said, holding out her hand to let him kiss it as he always did. 'Ten minutes won't deter the lady waiting for you, I'm sure.'

Alexander surrendered, laughing, settling himself next to Sophie on a couch in the drawing-room while Mrs Wainwright plied him with Earl Grey and anchovy toast and demanded details of the condition of Ilex Cottage.

'It's charming, Gran,' said Sophie, her eyes shining with enthusiasm. 'I'd never seen inside one of those cottages before. It's so compact and cosy, and with the right curtains and a few coats of paint——'

'Yes, yes, darling, spare us the details.' Mrs Wainwright laughed. 'Delighted though I am to know you approve, it's Alexander's professional opinion I'm anxious to hear.'

Alexander supplied it succinctly, then slanted a smile at Sophie. 'My secretary will send you documented confirmation, of course.'

It was almost half an hour later before he rose to leave, and, sent by Mrs Wainwright to see him off, Sophie thanked him for giving her lunch and for taking her to Willow Reach.

'It was nice of you to give up your Saturday,' she said, as she walked with him to the car.

Alexander folded his long legs into the driving seat, then gave her a very straight look. 'No hardship, Sophie. And just for the records, I'm not really dashing off to an evening of riotous debauchery with a member of your sex.'

Sophie's chin lifted. 'Your social life is nothing to do with me!'

'Nevertheless I thought I'd let you know I'm dining with George and Sally Huntley, and, more significantly, Sally's uncle, who just so happens to be on the board of directors of the hotel chain concerned with the site in Brading.'

Sophie's pleasure at hearing this surprised her so much, her voice sharpened with the effort to hide it. 'Don't you ever do things because you simply want to, Alexander, instead of always with an eye to business?'

'Why, yes.' His eyes gleamed beneath lowered lids. 'That's precisely what I've been doing all day today, up to now. Goodnight, little sister.' And with a mocking salute he sent the roadster purring down the drive to the road.

'That's a strange expression,' observed Mrs Wainwright when Sophie joined her. 'Alexander teasing you again?'

'Yes.' Not that Sophie was very sure. The look in Alexander's eyes had been hard to identify. If he had been any other man she would have sworn he was making a very clear statement of intent. But he wasn't anyone else. He was Alexander Paget, who had known her all her life, and who, more to the point, had been on the point of marrying Delphine only a short time before. This sudden rush of interest smacked too much of the rebound for Sophie's taste. Besides, Alexander's role in her life had always been rather like an extra brother. Not, Sophie thought broodingly, that fraternal seemed the right description for Alexander of late. His attitude was very disturbing, not least because she felt sure his objective was balm for the wounds Delphine had inflicted. She found she quite badly wanted to know which was affected most—his pride or his heart.

Cecily Wainwright made no comment on her granddaughter's abstraction, turning instead to the forthcoming wedding while they ate a light supper. She was amused when Sophie confessed her surprise at her father's news. 'You must be blind, child. Kate Paget's been in love with David for years.'

Sophie looked at her grandmother in astonishment. *'Really?'*

'Oh, nothing untoward! Kate was Louise's closest friend all her life, even bridesmaid at the wedding. Then Kate surprised everyone by suddenly marrying Hugh Paget only a few weeks later, a man years older than herself, who already had a son.' Mrs Wainwright's smile was confidential. 'Personally I was always convinced it was because your father chose Louise. Though, to be fair, "chose" was hardly the word.'

'Mother always said she and Dad took one look at each other and that was that.'

'Nothing your grandfather or I said made any difference, certainly. People didn't just live together in those days, you know, but Louise would have gone off with David like a shot if we'd opposed the marriage.' Mrs Wainwright's smile was wry. 'So we let her have her way. And then Kate married her widower and I swear to this day she did it because it meant staying near Louise—and David.'

Sophie stirred a spoon round and round in her coffee-cup. 'I wonder how it feels to love someone so much? I mean like Mother and Dad, and Aunt Kate, too, if she's been carrying a torch all these years. I'm not at all sure I want to feel so violently over anyone.'

'Have you never considered marrying Julian Brett?'

Sophie sighed impatiently. 'No, dearest of grandmothers, I have not. Julian's not the marrying kind. And, before you begin to nurture any ideas to the contrary, neither am I.'

'If you fell in love you'd probably think otherwise,' observed Mrs Wainwright mildly.

'So I'll make sure I keep both feet on the ground. If I ever detect even the slightest inclination in myself towards falling in love, I'll run like hell!'

'Sophie!'

Sophie apologised and for the rest of the weekend took care to avoid the subject, which was easy enough, since all she really wanted to talk about was Ilex Cottage. Her thoughts, however, were less exclusive. Excited though she was about moving into a place of her own, the look in Alexander's eyes as he drove off kept intruding on her visions of solitary bliss.

The following afternoon Sophie refused to allow her grandmother to drive her home, unwilling to let Mrs Wainwright drive sixty miles or so on a damp, foggy day. 'I shall go by bus,' she said firmly.

'But it stops at every lamp-post on the way, child,

you'll be ages getting home.' Mrs Wainwright paused, interrupted by the doorbell, and sent Sophie to open the front door.

Alexander stood outside, smiling down at her. 'Hello, Sophie. Thought you might fancy a lift home.'

Sophie stared at him, nonplussed. 'Did you come all this way just to fetch me?'

Alexander nodded affably. 'Of course I did. I'm really quite an obliging sort of fellow, you know.'

'You must be, to drive thirty miles just on the offchance. I was about to catch a bus.'

'Wouldn't you prefer my car?'

Sophie regarded him with a suspicion Alexander obviously found very amusing. 'I wish I knew what you're up to,' she said at last. 'This sudden rush of attention on your part is very worrying. You must have some ulterior motive. Come on, confess. What is it?'

'Nothing sinister,' he assured her smoothly. 'It's all part of my plan to unite the Pagets and Gordons in one happy family. My motives, I swear, are of the purest.'

Mrs Wainwright's appearance put paid to further argument until greetings had been exchanged, offers of tea refused, and Sophie was in the Mercedes on the way home to Deansbury, when she returned to the subject with persistence, telling Alexander his change of attitude was making her uneasy.

'It's spooky,' she said frankly. 'I don't like it. You've always been the boys' ally, not mine. In fact you and I have never hit it off all that well at all, really. At one time we never managed to exchange two words without disagreeing, then you moved into your superior phase——'

'My *what?*' he asked, startled.

'Your superior phase—dating roughly from the time you went off to college until, I suppose, right up to your wedding day.'

Alexander threw her a narrow, frowning look, then returned his concentration to the road, which was half obscured by floating trails of mist.

'Superior,' he repeated. 'Is that how you've thought of me all these years?'

'Yes. Not,' she added with brutal candour, 'that you've occupied my thoughts all that much, Alexander.'

'Why?'

'Why what?'

'Why *don't* I merit much thought from you, Sophie?'

His voice was so toneless that Sophie eyed his profile in surprise, wondering if he was annoyed.

'Well,' she began, sorry she'd ever embarked on the subject, 'I suppose it's because you're so self-contained and sickeningly successful at everything. I mean, at school you sailed through exams, you were cricket captain, head boy. And in adult life you've always been well liked and respected, with your niche in life all ready carved out for you in the family firm. You just never seem to suffer from petty things like the rest of us—I don't even remember your going through the spotty stage, like Tim and the twins.'

Alexander's laugh was short. 'Which only goes to show how effective those blinkers of yours are, Sophie. You don't remember the spots because you're years younger than I am, and my spots, if we must discuss them, just didn't register on you at the time. You probably failed to notice our respective parents were something more than just good friends because you've always been so wrapped up in your own particular form of martyrdom.'

Sophie shot upright in her seat. *'Martyrdom?'*

'That's right. I think you make rather a meal of the little paragon bit.'

There was a very tense silence in the car for some time as Sophie battled with the temper she rarely allowed herself to lose, because she knew from experience it did more harm to herself than to the object of her wrath.

'So that's how *you* see *me,*' she observed with hard-won calm. 'A sort of masochistic Cinderella, with handsome brothers instead of ugly sisters.'

'And I've decided to cast myself in the role of surrogate godfather,' he said casually. 'It's time you woke up to what's going on around you, Sophie —made the most of your life.'

'It's what I've been wanting to do for years,' she said, through gritted teeth. 'More to the point, it's exactly what I'm trying to do *now,* if I can ever manage to convince all of you I'm perfectly able to take care of myself.'

'You could have begun doing it some time ago if you'd ever woken up to the fact that David and Kate were only too ready to relieve you of your self-imposed domesticity.' Alexander reduced speed as he was talking, turning smoothly into a lay-by on the deserted road.

'Why have we stopped?' demanded Sophie,

alarmed.

'So you and I can have a little private chat.' Alexander turned towards her. 'Did you never realise that David hadn't the heart to hurt you by ousting you from your earth-mother syndrome until the need for it was past? Kate would have stepped in any time this past year or so, but she and David were afraid of hurting your feelings.'

'Not,' observed Sophie with feeling, 'a virtue one can attribute to you, Alexander Paget.'

'Which is probably why you and I disagreed so much when we were younger.'

'Very likely.' Sophie sagged in her seat, feeling utterly deflated. 'Why didn't *you* ever say anything, then, since you were so clued up about the entire situation?'

'Kate and David wouldn't hear of it. So, since it really wasn't any business of mine, I kept my mouth shut. And,' he added with candour, 'until just recently you weren't the constant focus of my attention. I was involved with Delphine by the time I realised how things stood with Kate.'

'Which meant you had no time to spare for irrelevant details like me.' Sophie managed a wry laugh. 'Not that I blame you. Delphine must have been an all-consuming interest.'

There was another of those silences Sophie had come to recognise as routine lately when alone with Alexander. This one was not thick with unspoken insults. It was surprisingly comfortable to sit alone with him in the gathering dusk.

'Delphine,' said Alexander after a while, 'was like an addiction, a habit I found hard to kick once it had

begun. I never saw enough of her for my enthusiasm
to pall, was never given enough physical satisfaction
for my appetite to——'

'Sicken and so die?'

'Exactly.' Alexander's voice dropped several
tones. 'Looking back on it, Sophie, I think I knew in
one part of me that marriage with Delphine had no
lasting chance of success.'

'The superior, above-the-belt Alexander. The rest
of you wanted her come hell or high water, I
suppose.'

Alexander sighed. 'Only, I suspect, because she
flatly refused to let me have her.'

'You mean you might not have married her if
she'd gone to bed with you as you wanted?'

Alexander was quiet for a moment. 'Sophie, I
honestly don't know. Anyway, the question's
academic—she didn't go to bed with me, and in the
end she didn't marry me, either, so now I'll never
know.'

'If she reappeared tomorrow and repented on both
counts, would you have her back?' asked Sophie.

'I'd be tempted,' he said frankly. 'But I hope I'd
have enough sense to refuse. She betrayed my trust,
and, if I may descend to the purely selfish for a
moment, she made me look like a bloody fool. I
don't know that I'd care to lay myself open to a
repeat performance. Not that the question arises. I
received a suitably penitent letter from her a few days
ago, saying how sorry she was and how she felt I was
too wonderful a man to have a wife who was secretly
hankering after the fame and success she's now all set
to enjoy.'

Sophie pulled a face in the darkness. 'Would you think me excessively catty if I said Delphine should have told you all that a jolly sight sooner?'

'No, not in the least. I agree.' Alexander felt for her hand and held it. 'But Terry Foyle didn't turn up with the bait until the eleventh hour, unfortunately.'

'Are you still suffering from—from the addiction you mentioned?' Sophie asked diffidently.

'No. It was cured by that hellish wait in the register office. Not to mention my unilateral honeymoon. Both very efficient remedies, Sophie.'

'Then it sounds as though your pride, rather than your heart, suffered most.'

Alexander's fingers tightened on hers. 'I knew Delphine for too short a time to sustain any lasting hurt.'

'I thought it only took a moment to fall in love!'

'And about the same to fall out of it—if it's only infatuation.' Alexander raised her fingers to his lips and, to Sophie's utter astonishment, kissed them one by one. 'The more enduring emotions—friendship, affection, warmth—grow and develop all the time in the right kind of relationship.'

Sophie drew her hand away. 'Alexander, I don't——'

'Don't what?' he said softly, and slid an arm behind her to gather her close as he kissed her mouth.

There was nowhere, Sophie soon realised, to retreat in the seat of a car like Alexander's roadster. As his mouth met hers her head fell back against the double support of Alexander's muscular arm and the headrest, while his free hand held her head still, so that movement of any kind was almost impossible.

One of her arms was trapped between his chest and hers, her legs were confined by the steering column, and, when her free hand went up to pull at his wrist, it was like tugging at an iron bar. She decided her best plan was to stay perfectly still and unresponsive. He would soon grow tired of trying to kiss a lifeless dummy. The plan proved to be a total failure, since she found herself growing less lifeless by the second. Her responses, Sophie discovered, were bent on functioning independently of her brain. In fact, after only a few more seconds of persuasion from Alexander's expert mouth Sophie's brain gave up altogether, and her lips parted in abrupt surrender.

Alexander made a muffled, relishing sound deep in his throat, and joined both arms around her. A minority section of her brain revived fleetingly to warn her that all this was highly inadvisable, that it would be Monday morning all too soon, and the man kissing her with such unprecedented enthusiasm was also the man who would be waiting for her behind his desk when she arrived to work for him the following day. The last-ditch attempt failed, and Sophie abandoned herself to the wholly unexpected pleasure she was receiving, *and* giving, if the quickened tempo of Alexander's breathing was anything to go by. At the first touch of his tongue in her mouth her own curled against it in response, and Alexander gave a stifled groan and raised his head momentarily, but only to move his lips to her heavy lids, closing them with kisses that moved over her face and down her throat, lingering on the pulse he found throbbing there.

Suddenly there was a glare of lights and a braying wail of sirens as two police cars careered past, shat-

tering the night with noise and lighting up the
darkness for a few intrusive moments that brought
Sophie back to earth with a bump. Before she had
time to push Alexander away he was upright and in
his former place, breathing very audibly as Sophie
gathered her scattered wits. She was suddenly very
angry—with him, with herself, and, most of all, she
realised, mortified, with the police cars for
interrupting them. She shivered, and Alexander
breathed in sharply.

'I'm sorry, Sophie.'

Sophie was not pleased to receive an apology. 'For
kissing me?' she demanded.

'Good God, no! How could I be sorry for something that gave me more pleasure than I imagined
possible?'

This question found even less favour. Why should
Alexander feel so surprised? Was it beyond the
bounds of possibility that kissing Sophie Gordon
could be such a pleasurable pastime?

'What exactly are you sorry for, then?' she asked.

Alexander recaptured her hand. 'Because we were
interrupted, because I gave in to the urge to make
love to you in just about the most uncomfortable
place possible, because, more than anything, I think,
I've known you so long and so well and have never
made love to you before.'

'Aren't you taking my part in all this rather for
granted?'

'Only in the light of your recent response, Sophie.'

'Oh.'

'Yes. Oh.' Alexander's voice grew husky. 'I never
dreamed so much fire lay hidden behind that dis-

ciplined exterior of yours.'

Sophie's eyes widened. 'Disciplined? Me?'

Alexander squeezed her hand. 'Yes. No one could live the sort of life you do without discipline, Sophie.'

'It doesn't come easy,' she informed him drily. 'Not even to paragons like me. I have to work hard at it.'

'I realise that. It's why the disciplined front is what most people accept, instead of the other Sophie tucked away behind it.'

'The one who yearns to escape!'

Alexander's grip tightened. 'Are you sure that a cottage overlooking the graveyard in Arlesford is the best means of escape, Sophie?'

'It's the best offer I've ever had, believe me!'

'You could always marry.'

Sophie sighed. 'As I keep saying, *ad nauseam,* I, better than anyone, know what marriage means. No, thanks.'

'But you're talking about the daily bread of domesticity, Sophie. Marriage could, and should, provide a lot of butter—*and* jam.'

'Alexander, if you mean what I think you mean, all I've ever lacked is an actual husband who, perfectly naturally, would expect to take me to bed and make love with me on top of all the rest.' She shook her head fiercely. 'No way.'

Alexander laughed. 'So not only do you eschew the delights of domesticity, you're ready to dismiss the pleasures of the bed.'

'I won't miss something I've never had.'

The now familiar silence fell for a few moments,

then Alexander reached a hand to flick on the interior light so he could look hard at Sophie's face. She scowled at him crossly.

'Turn the light off! I feel like a sitting duck.'

Afterwards the darkness seemed denser than before. 'I wanted to see if you meant it, Sophie,' he said quietly.

'That I've never been to bed with anyone?' She chuckled. 'But that's strictly between you and me, Alexander. I don't want it spread around. Think how my reputation would suffer!'

'I'm surprised. And don't try telling me you're frigid, because I proved conclusively just now that you're not.'

'What's so surprising about it?' she asked defensively. 'You said Delphine wouldn't let you into *her* bed.'

'But that's because she was holding out for a wedding ring. I'm not gullible enough to believe no one had shared her bed before.'

'Yet you still wanted her!'

'Of course I did. I'm not antediluvian enough to expect a woman with Delphine's looks to be a virgin at her age. Nor,' he added, 'to be frank, would I have expected it of you, either, Sophie.'

Sophie thought this over, uncertain whether she was flattered or not. 'Because I'm twenty-three, you mean?'

He laughed softly. 'No. Because you're a very beddable lady, whatever age you are.'

'Oh, come on!' she said scathingly. 'Laying it on a bit thick, Alexander.'

'What do you mean?' The surprise in his voice was

so genuine, Sophie squeezed the hand holding hers.

'Put it this way. Remember I said you were superior? I have this little game I like to play, categorising people with a single adjective. You know yours. So my grandmother's is "autocratic", my father's "conscientious", Tim's "ambitious", the twins—being twins—share "exhausting", Kate's is "loving"—and so on. Am I boring you?'

'Not in the least! I don't really relish my own label, but go on. What I want to know is how you describe yourself.'

'My passport says it all, really. Hair brown, eyes brown, no distinguishing marks. In a word, "average".' Sophie paused. 'Or maybe "ordinary", because certain of my statistics are rather more generous than average.'

Alexander's utter stillness made her shift uneasily in her seat.

'So you're ordinary, are you?' he remarked very softly.

'Yes. Depressingly so.'

'Wrong.' He sounded so positive, Sophie fidgeted even more. 'There's nothing ordinary about your eyes, for a start,' he said, in a rather clinical manner. 'They're big enough and bright enough, God knows, and they smile even when your mouth stays all prim and proper, when you're trying not to laugh. Your nose turns up a little, it's true, but only enough to look endearing, and your mouth——' He paused. 'If I'm honest, it is a little on the wide side, Sophie, but it curves very temptingly, and now I give the matter thought, there's a fullness about the bottom lip——'

'OK, Alexander,' she said hastily, snatching her

hand away. 'No need to go on and on.'

He recaptured her hand and slid his arm behind
her. 'I haven't finished yet.'

'Alexander——'

'Quiet,' he said sternly. 'I've only just started.'

Sophie wriggled frantically, but his arm tightened,
keeping her still. 'Alexander, it's time we went
home.'

'In a moment. I would just like to rid your head of
this "ordinary" nonsense.' His voice roughened
slightly. 'For one thing, as you say, there are certain
things about you that are well above average, take
my word for it.' And his hand released hers to move
over the contours of her breasts, sliding over the thin
wool of her shirt. He muttered indistinctly and
brought his mouth down on hers. Sophie gasped, her
breasts rising and hardening in response to the caress
of his fingers. He took his arm from behind her, his
mouth increasing its pressure so that her head fell
back against the headrest as he dealt summarily with
shirt buttons and the satin that lay beneath, pulling it
down so that her breasts were pushed above it, bare
and pointing, shamelessly offering themselves to
hands that took loving possession of the silk-smooth
fullness.

Sophie gave a smothered cry, trying to push him
away, but Alexander caught her hands and pulled
them wide, bending his head to take one of the
swollen peaks in his mouth. Her body flushed all
over with heat as his teeth grazed and his lips closed
over a nipple, sending waves of heat knifing through
her. Just as she thought she could bear it no more,
Alexander returned his mouth to hers, kissing her

parted lips with such demand that Sophie was vanquished.

When he raised his head at last, he said raggedly, 'Never say *ordinary* again, my modest little sexpot. It quite definitely doesn't apply.'

Sophie pulled herself together hastily and pushed him away, but her fingers trembled so much, Alexander was obliged to help button her shirt, his own hands gratifyingly shaky, she noticed. 'If I'm not ordinary, what am I, then?' she couldn't resist asking.

'If only one word is allowed, mine isn't an adjective.'

'Are you being rude?'

He cleared his throat as he switched on the ignition, turning his head to look at her before he drove off. 'No four-letter words, I assure you. The word that sprang to mind was "dynamite".'

CHAPTER SIX

SOPHIE was never enamoured of Monday at the best of times, but next morning she walked into Deansbury on leaden feet, deeply reluctant to face Alexander in the cold light of day. It was raining, and the pavements were treacherous with slick layers of fallen leaves as she trudged along her usual route to the market square, which was always fairly quiet at this time of day, with another half-hour to go before shops opened and the day got off to its real start. When she arrived at Paget & Sons Sophie put away her umbrella and hung up her wet raincoat, then fiddled with her hair and face until she could put off the evil hour no longer.

The encounter was less trying than expected. Perry was with Alexander, telling him about the new girl he'd met at a party, his blue eyes glittering as he waved his hands about to emphasise the importance of the occurrence.

'For God's sake, go away and channel your energies into some work. Dream up something spectacular to show the brewery for the new pub in Market Street,' said Alexander, looking up with a smile as Sophie appeared. 'Good morning, Sophie.'

'Good morning.' Her smile included both men and Perry gave her his usual spectacular grin before going off to do his cousin's bidding.

'It astonishes me that there are any girls left in the neighbourhood for Perry to discover,' said Alexander, and pulled the day's consignment of post towards him, plainly bent on getting on with the day at top speed, to Sophie's gratitude. The weekend might never have happened, she thought with relief, and concentrated on Alexander's voice, much comforted by the matter-of-factness of his manner. Indeed, apart from the hour they spent together each morning, she saw very little of Alexander that day or the next, since he spent most of the time in Arlesford, organising the new branch office.

'You won't forget the interviews today, will you?' she reminded him on the Wednesday morning. 'The first is at eleven.'

Alexander studied her broodingly. 'Can't wait to get away, can you?'

'I merely want to get things settled,' she said patiently. 'I've promised I won't go until the new secretary knows the ropes.'

'You haven't changed your mind, then?' He dropped his eyes to the pen he was rolling between his fingers.

Sophie backed away hurriedly. 'No, I haven't.' She returned to her own office quickly, uneasy at something in Alexander's voice, which was too reminiscent of Sunday's intimacy for her peace of mind.

Sophie had made a careful selection of candidates for Alexander's approval. The first girl was very pretty, but Sophie knew at once she would never pass muster because she had a shrill voice and ultra-long scarlet fingernails. The second candidate was innocent of nail-polish, make-up, and any attempt whatsoever to make herself attractive, however efficient she might have been, and Sophie mentally ticked her off the list as well.

Alexander strode into Sophie's office a little later and leaned his hands on her desk. 'Come and have lunch with me.'

'I've brought sandwiches.'

'Feed 'em to the birds.' The dark-lashed eyes took on a cajoling look Sophie associated more with the engaging Perry than his senior partner. 'Please, Sophie. Interviewing those women was a cold reminder that you'll soon be gone. Call it a working lunch if it makes you happier.'

Sophie wavered, then gave in. 'All right. But I'll meet you in the George in twenty minutes or so. I must finish this report first.'

Alexander's smile conveyed such genuine pleasure, Sophie felt flattered. And she wanted to have lunch with Alexander, if she was honest. After he'd left, whistling, she acknowledged secretly that she'd enjoyed lunching with him the previous Saturday. Her fingers halted in their flight over the keys. This new, attentive Alexander was a difficult man to resist, she found, her stomach muscles tightening as she thought, not for the first time, of the episode in his car. She had enjoyed his lovemaking far more than she cared to admit, even to herself, and put her responses down to the fact that she was a normal, healthy female, and Alexander was a very attractive man. Any woman would have behaved similarly under the same circumstances.

Even so, Sophie was in no way prepared for the surge of delight she experienced as she entered the bar of the George a little later and saw Alexander spring to his feet at the sight of her. His wave and smile was noted and commented on by all present, she knew only too well, as she made her way through the usual lunch-time crush to join him on the far side of the room.

'Tell me the worst,' she said, as she sipped the wine he had ready for her. 'I suppose I can write a couple of polite rejections to this morning's candidates?'

Alexander agreed gloomily. 'You suppose right. I didn't bother to send them out for a test because I knew damn well I could never stand either of those two round me all day and every day.'

'Perhaps one of this afternoon's ladies will be suitable.' Sophie gave him a mischievous smile. 'I should have asked for photographs. You could have chosen the ones you fancied most.'

Alexander refused to cheer up. 'Whatever she looks like, your successor will have a hard act to follow.'

Sophie felt startled. 'Why, thank you, Alexander. How kind of you to say so.'

'It's the truth.' Alexander looked up to meet her eyes. 'I shall miss you badly, Sophie. Won't you change your mind?'

'Is that why you asked me to lunch? To persuade me?' Sophie's tone was cold, to hide her sudden urge to give in and tell him she'd stay.

'No. I just wanted your company. Is that so hard to believe?'

Sophie wanted to believe. It was disquieting to find she wanted to believe everything Alexander said these days, not least the previous Sunday when he'd disagreed so gratifyingly with her own view of herself as Miss Ordinary. 'Sorry, Alexander. I didn't mean to be prickly.'

His smile brought the colour to her face. 'The most fragrant roses sport the sharpest thorns, don't they? You're blushing, Sophie,' he added.

'Is it any wonder?' she snapped, glad of the diversion as plates were set before them, and Alexander began to talk shop. For the remainder of their time together they discussed the new branch office, his ideas on furnishing Willow Reach, with a few minutes spent, inevitably, on discussing Ilex Cottage and how soon it would be fit for occupation.

'Not that I need wait for that before I move to Arlesford,' she said. 'I can always live at Greenacre if Mr Jefford wants me sooner.'

'Jefford can wait until I can do without you,' said Alexander flatly.

Sophie frowned. 'And how long is that going to be, may I ask?'

Alexander leaned his chin on his hand, his eyes almost concealed by his enviably thick lashes. 'That, Miss Gordon, is something I'm beginning to worry about a great deal.'

Her dark eyes opened wide. 'Surely another month will be long enough?'

'We'll have to wait and see,' he said cryptically, and helped her on with her coat.

The two applicants who arrived in the afternoon were far more promising, one an attractive young woman in her thirties, the other a very pleasant lady with grey hair and a no-nonsense look about her. Both women were sent out to Sophie's office to demonstrate their efficiency at typing, and after the second lady had taken her leave Sophie rushed into Alexander's office to demand a verdict.

'Well?' she asked. 'Any good?'

'Your eagerness is scarcely flattering,' he said acidly, 'but I suppose I must admit that both women were excellent.'

'So which one do you want?'

Alexander turned from the window to look at her broodingly. 'You know that already, Sophie. I want you. But since I may not have you, I think the most sensible choice is Mrs Rogers, the widow.'

Sophie ignored the sudden leap of her pulse at his first words in her relief to hear his approval of the pleasant Mrs Rogers.

'I'm sure she'll be excellent,' she assured him.

'And unlikely to find Perry chasing her round her typewriter, either,' agreed Alexander.

'*I've* never had any trouble on that score!'

'For reasons previously explained.' Alexander came swiftly round the desk to take her by the shoulders. 'I laid the law down originally for our respective families' sakes. Now——' He paused, looking down deep into her eyes. 'Now I think my motives might be altogether more personal.'

'Shall I go out and come in again?' asked a patient voice behind them, and Alexander relinquished a very hot and bothered Sophie to explain to Perry that a new secretary had been found.

'And is she young and nubile?' Perry gave Sophie an outrageous wink as she passed him on her way out.

'Sorry, old chap,' drawled Alexander. 'Grey-haired widow-lady with sons older than you.'

'Thank God for that,' said Perry piously. 'It'll be nice to come in here without having to knock first.'

Sophie fled, feeling the sooner she left Paget & Sons, the better all round.

Over dinner that night Dr Gordon reiterated his worries about Ilex Cottage as a suitable home for his daughter. 'I only hope you won't be too lonely there, Sophie,' he said, his eyes anxious. 'Silly, I suppose, but I can't help worrying. I shall miss you, pet.'

'That's what Alexander said, too,' answered Sophie, rather wishing she hadn't as David Gordon's eyes narrowed. 'But he won't for long, of course. We found a replacement for me today.'

'So you'll be able to fly the nest quite soon, then.' Dr Gordon went on eating his dinner, looking dubious. 'But Ilex Cottage won't be ready for a while, will it?'

'No, but I can lodge at Greenacre while I finish the decorating and make curtains, and so on. Dad— could I take my own bed with me, do you think?'

She was assured she could take anything from the house she wanted, and jumped up to hug him affectionately.

'Unless you'd like new things,' he said. 'I think I can spare the pennies for a few sticks of furniture.'

Sophie assured him Ilex Cottage would look odd with contemporary things. 'Gran says I can have one or two pieces from Greenacre, too, so I'll be fine. It's such a minute place I shan't need much.'

There were less disturbing encounters with Alexander for a while, since Sophie flatly refused to lunch with him more than once a week, and took to spending every weekend with her grandmother so she could get on with her home-decorating in Ilex Cottage, leaving Kate to show prospective buyers over the Gordon home. The sale had been put in the hands of Sam Jefford, rather to Sophie's surprise. He came to measure the house himself, and afterwards rather diffidently suggested a meal somewhere the following evening, since they would soon be working together. Sophie agreed, finding she enjoyed her evening with him more than expected. Sam Jefford was restful company, a complete contrast with either Julian or Alexander. Time spent socially with Alexander smacked of armed truce these days, full of unsaid words and fraught with the feeling that any moment he might brush aside the barrier she tried to keep between them. Julian, on the other hand, took her for granted, Sophie knew, and she was quite untroubled by the fact.

Consequently, Sam Jefford's eagerness to please was rather refreshing. Sophie suspected it stemmed from his recent harrowing experience of divorce. He was lonely and showed it. It was an interesting pastime to analyse the differences in all three men while dining with Sam Jefford, or during a trip to the theatre with Julian. It was disturbing, however, to realise that during any time spent with Alexander, in work or out of it, she never gave a thought to either of the other men. Or to anyone else. Which made Sophie sorry she had promised to remain at home with her father until the wedding. It was high time she was up and away. It just wouldn't do to go any further down the path she seemed to be travelling with Alexander these days, because she was convinced that only heartbreak could lie at the end of it. Once she had made the break and left Deansbury, everything would be better, she told herself. On her own in Ilex Cottage, she would be safe.

'I hear you've been seen dining with a new man lately,' said Alexander one morning.

'Getting to know my new boss,' said Sophie.

'Not *too* well, I trust?'

'As well as advisable between employer and employee.' Sophie met his cool green gaze serenely.

Alexander, who was dressed for London in a dark overcoat and sober grey suit, gathered up his brief-case and strode to the door. 'For the first time I feel pleased that you're leaving me, Sophie.'

She stared at him, affronted.

'No insult intended,' he assured her, with a distinctly tigerish smile. 'Since you seem to set limits on professional relationships, I look forward to the day when your relationship with *me,* Sophie, will be a purely personal one.' He gave her a brief ironic bow and departed for his conference, leaving Sophie completely routed.

Alexander's absence gave Sophie a golden opportunity to give Mrs Rogers a teach-in on the routine at Paget & Sons. The new secretary was a quick study, and showed signs of proving highly satisfactory. Her keen sense of humour gave her a head start with Perry, her interest in his children quickly endeared her to George Huntley, while the young draughtsmen and trainees were her slaves from the start because Mrs Rogers brought batches of home-made cakes to serve at coffee-time.

'One up on you, Sophie,' remarked Perry, mouth

PLAY
HARLEQUIN'S

LUCKY HEARTS

GAME

AND YOU COULD GET

★ **FREE BOOKS**
★ **A FREE BRACELET WATCH**
★ **A FREE SURPRISE GIFT**
★ **AND MUCH MORE**

**TURN THE PAGE AND
DEAL YOURSELF IN** →

PLAY "LUCKY HEARTS" AND YOU COULD GET...

★ Exciting Harlequin Presents® novels—FREE
★ A bracelet watch—FREE
★ A surprise mystery gift that will delight you—FREE

THEN CONTINUE YOUR LUCKY STREAK WITH A SWEETHEART OF A DEAL

When you return the postcard on the opposite page, we'll send you the books and gifts you qualify for, absolutely free! Then, you'll get 8 new Harlequin Presents® novels every month, delivered right to your door months before they're available in stores. If you decide to keep them, you'll pay only $2.24★ per book—that's 26 cents below the cover price and there is no extra charge for postage and handling! You can cancel at any time by marking "cancel" on your statement or returning a shipment to us at our cost.

★ Free Newsletter!

You'll get a free newsletter—an insider's look at our most popular authors and their upcoming novels.

★ Special Extras—Free!

When you subscribe to the Harlequin Reader Service®, you'll also get additional free gifts from time to time as a token of our appreciation for being a home subscriber.

★Terms and prices subject to change without notice.
Sales tax applicable in NY and Iowa.
© 1989 HARLEQUIN ENTERPRISES LIMITED

HARLEQUIN'S

With a coin — scratch off the silver card and check below to see how many gifts you get.

YES! I have scratched off the silver card. Please send me all the books and gifts for which I qualify. I understand that I am under no obligation to purchase any books, as explained on the opposite page.

108 CIH CAPE (U-H-P-12/89)

NAME

ADDRESS   APT.

CITY   STATE   ZIP

Twenty-one gets you 4 free books, a free bracelet watch and mystery gift

Twenty gets you 4 free books and a free bracelet watch

Nineteen gets you 4 free books

Eighteen gets you 2 free books

DETACH AND MAIL CARD TODAY

HARLEQUIN "NO RISK" GUARANTEE

★ You're not required to buy a single book—ever!
★ As a subscriber, you must be completely satisfied or you may cancel at any time by marking "cancel" on your statement or returning a shipment of books at our cost.
★ The free books and gifts you receive from this LUCKY HEARTS offer remain yours to keep—in any case.

full one day. 'Why have *you* never made cake for us?'

Sophie told him bluntly that no cake she made ever got past Matt and Mark, and now they were away she saw no point in adding to either her father's waistline or her own. Perry regarded the area in question and gave his opinion of her shape in terms that made her blush, adding that his wasn't the only eye in the office which took pleasure in dwelling on her charms.

'Only for God's sake don't tell Alexander I said so,' he begged. 'Himself is incredibly touchy where you're concerned these days. A touch of the green-eye, would you say? A scalp too many dangling at your belt of late?'

Sophie's dignified rebuttal was rather impaired by being called to the telephone to Sam Jefford, whose request for her company at lunch sounded untypically urgent.

'Is it all right if I go off to lunch a little early?' she asked reluctantly, self-conscious under Perry's mischievous blue gaze. 'Mrs Rogers will hold the fort for me.'

'Off you go, darling.' He wagged his finger. 'While the cat's away, and all that.'

Sam Jefford was waiting for Sophie in a quiet tea-shop well away from the market square, an establishment rarely patronised by the businessmen of the town. Sophie had chosen it deliberately, not happy about the ethics of lunching with her new employer in the George while she was still employed by Alexander. Not, she assured herself, that it was any business of the latter. Nor was her choice of rendezvous influenced by the desire to meet Sam

Jefford unseen by anyone she knew. But she was worried about what had brought him thirty miles to see her in the middle of a working day.

Her apprehension increased the moment she saw Sam. He wore an aura of uneasiness about him, despite the diffident charm of his smile.

'Hello,' she said cordially, as she joined him. 'What brings you to Deansbury at this time of day? Business?'

'Certainly not pleasure, Sophie.' He stared unseeingly at the menu.

'The Welsh rarebit's quite good here,' she said gently.

He pushed the menu aside. 'I'm really not very hungry. I'll just have some coffee, I think.'

Sophie smiled encouragingly. 'Snags with the sale of the house?'

'No.' He met her eyes with a desperate look. 'I've struck a snag in quite another area, actually. With my secretary.'

Sophie's heart sank. 'Oh, dear.'

He swallowed convulsively, staring down into the coffee the waitress put in front of him. 'I feel so bad about all this, but, well, you see the girl who works for me now——'

'The pregnant lady.'

'Quite. Well, I automatically assumed she would be leaving for good, you see. But she isn't. I mean, she doesn't want to. She wants to come back after the baby's born.'

Sophie regarded his downbent head in silence. 'You didn't know?'

He looked up miserably. 'I'm pretty hopeless

where women are concerend. It seems she expected to all along—she's not married, you see. She needs the job—even has a sister who'll fill in until she gets back.'

Sophie reached across and patted his hand. 'Don't worry, Sam.' She smiled a little. 'I'll find something else.'

He covered the hand with his own. 'Does this mean you'll stop seeing me now? Socially, I mean?'

'Of course not.' Sophie finished her coffee and stood up. 'Anyway, I'd better get back now. I'll give you a ring when I'm settled in Ilex Cottage. You can come round for a drink, or something.'

Sam Jefford followed her outside, looking forlorn. She smiled at him cheerfully, bade him a brisk goodbye and made her way back to Paget's, feelig forlorn herself. What on earth was she to do now? she thought in dismay.

Dr Gordon was very definite with his views when she told him later that the new job in Arlesford had fallen through. He strongly disapproved of his daughter's taking off to live alone with no job prospect.

'Since you've been in such a tearing hurry to organise your own replacement at Paget's,' he said forcibly, 'you'd better stay with Kate and me at the Chantry until you find yourself something to do in reach of Ilex Cottage.'

Sophie could have wept. Instead she swallowed hard on her response to this unusually dictatorial pronouncement and prepared herself for an evening devoted to answering the telephone, because it was Dr Gordon's night on call, with the added delights of preparing a casserole for the next day and tackling a pile of ironing, none of which came into her top ten of favourite occupations. Her father was called out before he'd had time to swallow his coffee, leaving Sophie alone to ponder bitterly on the irony of fate which gave out with one hand and took back with the other. Mrs Rogers had proved so instantly efficient that Sophie had taken the plunge and informed Perry she was leaving the following Friday, which meant only another week at her present salary. Alexander was a very fair employer who expected his pound of flesh, but also expected to pay generously for the privilege, and Sophie had amassed a comforting little nest egg. But it had been meant for such contingencies as new curtains and carpets for Ilex Cottage, not for tiding her over until, or if, she found a new job.

Sophie answered the telephone several times during the evening, sometimes to a worried patient, sometimes to her father, who usually called in to check where he was needed next. The list was larger than usual, enough to keep Dr Gordon occupied all evening due to the distances involved in reaching patients in outlying districts, and Sophie had prepared her casserole and was half-way through the ironing when the doorbell rang. She sighed, hoping it was not some patient local enough to call on her father in person, then stared in astonishment as she found Alexander on the doorstep, looking tired and pale, dressed in the clothes he'd worn to London.

'May I come in?' he asked.

'Of course.' Sophie fought down a surge of excitement at the sight of him and led the way through to the kitchen. 'Do you mind if I carry on ironing?' she said, glancing up at him curiously as she renewed her attack on the pile of shirts. 'Something wrong, Alexander?'

He watched her, the glare of the strip light striking sparks of gold from his thick fair hair, and emphasising the marks of fatigue beneath his eyes and the silver-gilt stubble on his jaw.

'I called in at the office before going home, Sophie. Perry left me a memo with various bits of information, the most important of which was the news that you're leaving next week.'

Fool that I am, thought Sophie. She nodded. 'Yes. Mrs Rogers is an absolute marvel, so I couldn't see the point of staying longer. She's coming in again a couple of days beforehand for the changeover.'

'I see.' Alexander subsided on one of the tall stools. 'Jefford's getting impatient, I suppose.'

Sophie folded a shirt carefully. 'Not exactly. It seems I counted my chickens far too soon. Sam Jefford came over to Deansbury today to tell me his secretary wants her job back once her baby's born. She's not married and needs the money. So, I shall have to start job-hunting; very good for me, I suppose. A new experience.'

Alexander slid off the stool and unplugged the iron, then took her by the hands. 'I could offer you an alternative, Sophie.'

She stared up at him in surprise, her pulse beginning to race as she she met the molten gleam in his green eyes. Her breathing quickened and she ran the tip of her tongue over suddenly dry lips as the hurried movement of her breasts drew Alexander's gaze like a magnet.

'Sophie——' His voice was hoarse as he pulled her against him and kissed her fiercely, one arm almost cracking her ribs, his free hand moving over her breasts as his tongue slid into her mouth. Sophie yielded to him with a helpless moan, her arms sliding under his jacket to hold him closer, and he flattened his hand on the base of her spine, locking her hips against his as he pulled her on tiptoe against him.

Breathing like a marathon runner, Alexander picked her up and stood with her cradled in his arms, his mouth demanding a response Sophie answered without reserve. She locked her arms round his neck, returning his kisses fiercely, submerged in her own delirium, until at last Alexander gently lowered her to her bare feet once more. Contact with the cold quarry tile of the kitchen floor brought Sophie very literally back to earth. Alexander smiled crookedly, and smoothed her tumbled hair, touched his finger to her swollen bottom lip.

'Why did I never dream you'd be so inflammatory, I wonder?'

Sophie tried hard to control her breathing. 'I could say the same thing,' she muttered.

'Then it's mutual? I'm not fantasising about this—this explosion every time I touch you?'

'No,' she said grudgingly.

'You don't enjoy it?'

'I didn't say that.'

Alexander perched on the stool, drawing her close to stand between his outstretched legs. Sophie fidgeted, very much aware that neither of them had recovered from their heated exchange. 'Sophie,' he said quietly, 'I mentioned earlier I had an alternative proposition to make. Aren't you curious to hear what it is?'

Sophie bit her lip, almost certain she knew what he was going to say. The pieces of the jigsaw all fitted together so neatly. This sudden, newfound chemistry between them, her lack of a job, Alexander still smarting from his treatment at Delphine's hands. She was afraid it all added up to a proposal of marriage she didn't want. She wanted Alexander, it was true, but not Alexander on the rebound. She wanted, she realised with burning clarity, to go to bed with Alexander right this minute. Her body ached with frustration just from standing between the two rigid thighs keeping her prisoner. But Kate Paget's stepson could never ask Dr Gordon's only daughter to leap into bed with him—not without marrying her first.

'That's a very analytical look,' teased Alexander. 'Are you trying to guess what I have in mind?'

Sophie was unhappily certain what he had in mind. 'I think so, Alexander, but please—I don't want——'

'Hey!' He shook her slightly. 'Wait until you hear my proposition, at least, before you turn it down! Nothing sinister, I promise. I merely thought that now the job with Sam Jefford has fallen through you might care to carry on working for me instead.'

CHAPTER SEVEN

SOPHIE'S face went blank with astonishment, while Alexander's eyes narrowed to a very unsettling gleam.

'You *didn't* know what I had in mind, did you?' He put a finger under her chin. 'Sophie Gordon! Did you by any chance imagine I was about to request entry into your bed?'

'Yes,' lied Sophie faintly, weak with relief. Dear God, how close she'd come to making a complete and utter fool of herself. She offered up a silent prayer of thanks and gave Alexander a weak smile. 'Sorry.'

He shrugged ruefully. 'Don't apologise. If you were anyone else under these particular circumstances we'd be in bed at this very moment, finishing what we started. But you are your father's daughter——'

'And you're Aunt Kate's stepson,' Sophie finished for him.

'Which makes not a blind bit of difference to the fact that I want you like hell just the same,' said Alexander with intensity.

'But *why?*' Sophie's question was deeply curious. 'I'm just the same Sophie I've always been.'

'If I knew why, perhaps I'd be able to *stop* wanting you! I'm on a losing wicket, one way and another.

Knowing I can't have you makes me want you even more.'

'Just the same as Delphine.'

'Oh, no.' Alexander drew her closer. 'Not remotely the same as Delphine, since you mention it. For one thing, I was never allowed to make her untidy——'

'Spare me the sordid details!' Sophie struggled to wrench free, but his legs scissored to hold her prisoner as he jerked her against him.

'You brought it up. I'm just trying to make things clear.'

One thing was very clear to Sophie. Standing between his muscular thighs, pulled close to him as she was, it was impossible to ignore how much he wanted her. The hard, pulsing proof of it burned against her, right through faded denim and finest bespoke wool suiting.

'Alexander——' she gasped.

'Sophie,' he whispered in echo, and with a sudden show of strength lifted her off her feet and sat her on his lap, holding her still, ignoring her efforts to break free. 'I thought I wanted Delphine. God knows, she's beautiful enough. With you it's different. Very different.' The passionate sincerity of his voice quieted her as he cradled her against him, gazing down into her eyes as though willing her to see he was speaking the truth. 'You're *not* beautiful. But the way you look is a complete irrelevance. Sophie. It doesn't matter a damn whether you're dressed like this, or armoured in that no-nonsense stuff you wear to the office, or even with a red nose and swollen eyes like the night I made you so angry you threw up. I still burn with the same urge to pick you up and carry you off.'

'Where?' asked Sophie, fascinated.

His smile raised the tiny hairs all the way down her spine. 'I'm not sure—I rather think it's to my cave.'

The telephone interrupted the moment of danger, making them both jump. Alexander cursed and Sophie slid to the floor to answer it, unsteady on her feet from the effect of the new, uninhibited urges she had gone through life until recently believing were other women's prerogatives.

'Are you all right?' asked her father.

Sophie cleared her throat. 'Yes, Dad. Fine. No more calls.'

'Great. One more to go and I'll be home.'

Alexander followed her into the hall, shrugging into his overcoat. 'I'd better be off, hadn't I?' he said ruefully. 'Before I do, can I have an answer on the job question?'

'But, Alexander, you can't tell Mrs Rogers you've changed your mind—and you don't need *two* secretaries.'

'Ah, but I do. How about the new branch in Arlesford?'

Sophie's eyes lit like lamps. 'Oh, Alexander—do you mean it?'

'Of course I mean it! Why do you think I went out of my way to come here tonight?' he demanded, then smiled wryly. 'Which is not the whole truth and nothing but the truth, if I'm honest. I hoped I'd catch you alone.'

Sophie's eyes slid away from his. 'I could have been out.'

'Kate told me you always stay in when David's on call.'

'I might not have been alone.'

'True.' He shrugged and lounged against the newel post. 'To go on with what I was saying, you know Perry will run the branch in time, but in the beginning I'll need to get it off the ground myself. And I'll need an experienced secretary with me, one who can work on her own at times right from the start, since naturally I shall have to divide my time between Arlesford and Deansbury. In short, I need *you*, Sophie.'

Sophie threw her arms round him impulsively, tipping her head back to smile at him radiantly. 'I accept, Alexander—with gratitude.'

He smiled in mock-amazement. 'Why, thank you, Sophie. I'm not used to such appreciation from *you*.'

'While you've always had far too much from other women!' she said, grinning, then sobered. 'But I meant it, Alexander. I really am grateful. I was so miserable before you came because Dad had been laying the law down about my staying with him and Aunt Kate until I found a job in Arlesford. And I couldn't argue because he hardly ever comes the heavy father with me.' She pulled a face. 'I didn't relish the prospect of playing gooseberry to a couple of newlyweds.'

Alexander laughed, and bent to kiss her cheek. 'Well, now you won't have to. I told you I'd taken on the role of your guardian angel.'

Sophie looked at him thoughtfully for a moment. 'One thing, though. I really do want the job in Arlesford very much, but—how can I put it?—I mean it must be on a strictly business footing.' She flushed. 'Oh, lord, that sounds so big-headed. What I'm trying to say——'

'Is that I must not presume on your gratitude,' he said solemnly. 'No fun and games in the office, you mean.'

'I wouldn't have put it quite like *that*. I'm just asking that we work together as we've always done.'

'Of course. But on one condition. That you still let me help decorate your beloved cottage.'

She laughed. 'Don't worry—I turn no one away with paintbrush in hand.'

'Ah, but I insist on sole rights to the job.' And with a glint of green eyes Alexander bade her goodnight and went off, leaving Sophie in such a state of euphoria she had finished all the ironing and had a tray ready with coffee and sandwiches when her father eventually arrived home to hear the glad news.

Julian Brett struck the only discordant note in Sophie's life in the days that followed, surprising her not a little by his depression over her imminent departure.

'But you've known for ages that I was going, Julian,' she said, taken aback by his air of gloom as they dined together in Julian's favourite Italian restaurant.

Julian Brett was a slender man of thirty, with a pale face and a lot of soft dark hair. He was the curator of the Deansbury museum and lived with his mother in a large, antique-filled Victorian house only a stone's throw from where they were sitting at that moment. He refilled Sophie's wineglass and leaned back in his chair, studying her with lachrymose eyes.

'But I thought you were going to work for this Jefford chap,' he said.

Sophie drank her wine, feeling irritable. 'I told you it fell through, Julian. And if Alexander hadn't come to my rescue with the job at his new branch in Arlesford I'd have been forced to stay here until I found something else.'

'At least you'd have been safely under your father's roof,' he pointed out. 'And we could have carried on as usual.'

'Oh, really, Julian, the *status quo* may be the be all and end all of your existence, but *I* happen to yearn for change.'

'As I see it, Sophie, the only change in your life will be the fact that you live in that decrepit cottage instead of here.' His mouth thinned. 'Otherwise your working day will be dominated by Alexander the Great as usual!'

'Don't be feline.' Sophie frowned at him. 'You happen to like living at home with your mother, but I, love my family though I may, can't wait to have a little place of my own. All to myself,' she added, to remove any possible doubt.

Julian fiddled with his coffee spoon and cleared his throat several times before saying rather desperately, 'You could always have married *me,* Sophie.' He kept his eyes on the chequered tablecloth, which was just as well, since the blank astonishment in Sophie's face could hardly have been described as flattering.

'But Julian,' she said gently, 'you don't want to get married.'

'I don't want to lose you, either.' He looked up in

appeal. 'I mean, Mother won't live for ever, and you've never shown any signs of marrying anyone else. In fact you've always said you never wanted children, which is fine by me. Won't you at least consider it?'

Sophie could hardly believe her ears. 'But Julian—you're not in the least interested in having a wife!'

'I'm interested in having *you* for a wife, Sophie,' he assured her, with more urgency than she had ever heard in his voice. 'We could go on as we've always done. Mother would be pleased to have you move in with us, I'm sure. She gets lonely, you know, and she's quite fond of you. And there'd be no housekeeping to worry you—the Baxters have been with us for years.'

Sophie searched hard for a way to couch her refusal in suitably inoffensive terms. 'It's really very sweet of you, Julian, but you know better than anyone that I've never had marriage in mind—not even the kind you're proposing.' It hardly seemed charitable to tell him that the picture he painted of their future life together aroused a strong urge in her to turn tail and run out of the restaurant. Instead she enlarged on her appreciation of the offer, pointing out that Arlesford was only thirty miles away, that Julian could drive over and see her now and then once she was settled in at Ilex Cottage.

Julian looked at her aghast. 'My dear Sophie, you can't expect me to drive sixty miles or more in one evening just to take you out for a meal!'

Julian never took her out anywhere other than in Deansbury itself, in places where they could expect to encounter most of the upwardly mobile population of the prosperous town, Sophie reminded herself, resisting the urge to assault her escort with the Chianti bottle. It came as less surprise to her, therefore, than it would have to others to learn that by insisting on her move to Arlesford she had placed herself beyond Julian Brett's particular pale.

The following evening was a complete contrast. After Sophie's last day at the Deansbury branch of Pagets, the entire staff gave her a lively farewell dinner at the George Hotel, an evening much more to her taste than the one with Julian. Perry was on form, as usual, keeping the entire company entertained, while Alexander, as host, oversaw the smooth running of the evening in his own effortless way, attentive to Sophie in an understated manner no one took for anything different from usual. Only Sophie was conscious of an extra nuance; the added electricity which dated from the day of Alexander's return from Greece, something which seemed to grow and intensify each time they were alone together. All week at the office Alexander had been satisfactorily circumspect, apart from an occasional errant gleam in his eyes when they were alone, designed specifically, she knew, to give her an unnecessary reminder about the change in their relationship. But, as he sat beside her at the dinner-table, Alexander's thigh brushed Sophie's too often for coincidence, and each time the contact aroused a shock of response which surged through her entire body. The effort to hide it from the world at large filled her with illicit excitement, adding an edge to an evening she would have enjoyed to the full anyway,

even without the added bonus of sitting close to
Alexander.

He drank very little, she noticed.

'You're very abstemious tonight,' she commented
in an undertone.

'For a very good reason. I'm driving you home.'
He looked very deliberately at her mouth, then away
from her suddenly flushed face to press Sally
Huntley, his partner's wife, to more coffee.

At the end of the evening Perry sprang up to
propose a toast, listing Sophie's attributes with his
customary verve.

As everyone rose to echo the toast Sophie sat with
a lump in her throat, her cheeks poppy-red and her
eyes very bright, finding it hard to keep her voice
steady as she got up in response to cries of 'Speech!'
She thanked everyone for the exquisite jardinière,
told them how happy she'd been at the Deansbury
office, and how delighted she was at the prospect of
keeping in touch by means of the new Arlesford
branch. She turned very deliberately to Alexander.
'And last, but very definitely not least, I wish to
thank our host for an evening I'll always look back
on with immense pleasure.'

'That was a loaded remark you made at the end,'
commented Alexander as he drove her home.

'I was just being polite!'

'I'm sure everyone else thought so. My own
impression was different.'

'Do you deny you were—well, touching me under
the table all night?'

'No. You said I was to keep my distance during
office hours. Which I have,' he added virtuously.

'You didn't include social occasions in the taboo.'

'Then I should have. I was like a cat on hot bricks all evening!'

'You didn't show it.'

'But you knew very well how you were affecting me, didn't you?' she accused.

'The same way you were affecting me, I hope.' Alexander stopped the car a short distance from the house. 'There you are, Sophie. Home safe and sound.'

'Will you come in for coffee?'

'Is your father likely to be up?'

'Yes.'

'Then forgive me, but I won't. I'm not sure I can cope with more frustration tonight.'

Sophie stared down at her clasped hands. 'Then I'd better go in. Thank you for this evening and for bringing me home.' She reached up and kissed his cheek, and at once his arms shot out to hold her and his mouth closed hungrily on hers. When he raised his head he was breathing hard.

'I had almost persuaded myself I could let you go without doing that,' he muttered against her mouth. 'See what you reduce me to, Sophie Gordon—making love in cars like an importunate schoolboy.'

'I don't try to,' she whispered. 'I just can't get used to the fact that you—that I——'

'That two old friends like us should suddenly find they don't want to be friends, after all.'

Sophie drew away. 'Aren't we friends any more, then, Alexander?'

He gave a smothered laugh. 'Dammit, Sophie, surely it must be painfully obvious that I want to be your lover, not your friend!' His voice grated as he drew her back against him and began kissing her once more, and for a few wild moments her arms went round his neck, clutching him closer, then with superhuman effort Sophie tore herself away, gasping for breath.

'I must go in, Alexander. I can't stand much more of this. I'm just not used to it.'

He caught her hand. 'I'm sorry, Sophie. I didn't mean to break your rules. I promise I'll do my darnedest to toe the line when you start at the new office.'

Sophie squeezed his fingers. 'I was the one to blame. I shouldn't have kissed you. I promise I won't do it again.'

'Don't say that, Sophie——' He lifted her hand and kissed the palm, turning her fingers over to cover the place he'd kissed. 'Shall I see you this weekend?'

'Let's not make any prearranged plans, Alexander.'

'Why not?'

Sophie found it hard to explain why not. It sounded so pontifical to say she needed to leave home and start her new life, distancing herself from everything for a while before she could contemplate Alexander in the light of a lover. Because that was what he'd be if they saw much more of each other alone, she recognised with honesty. And it would be a very tricky relationship to maintain in secret, that was patently obvious, when their lives were so closely interlinked.

'Not yet,' she said with difficulty. 'It's too soon.'

'Too soon! We've known each other for twenty-odd years. How well do you have to know someone before you let them wine and dine you, for God's sake?'

'Don't be angry, Alexander. If you must know, I think it's too soon after Delphine.'

He let out a deep breath. 'Ah, I see. You still think I'm on my ego-boosting trip.'

Sophie thought it over. 'I did think so at first, I'll admit. Now I'm not so sure. Anyway, I still need some breathing space.'

'Fair enough,' said Alexander, suddenly brisk. 'I'll give you until our respective parents' wedding. After that . . .' He paused significantly. 'After that I expect a change of attitude, Sophie.'

'You mean you expect me to hop into bed with you the moment my father's back is turned?' she enquired acidly.

'No, I do not!' Alexander turned in his seat and took her by the shoulders, shaking her slightly. 'All I have in mind is an occasional dinner together or an evening at the theatre. More or less what you've been doing for years with Julian Brett——' He stopped short, staring down at her intently in the darkness. 'Or is *he* the stumbling block? You prefer his company to mine, possibly?'

The anger in his voice did wonders for Sophie's ego. 'Nothing to do with Julian,' she assured him. 'He's not prepared to travel as far as Arlesford to continue with our usual arrangement, you see.'

Alexander's shoulders shook. 'Good God! Not that I'm surprised in a way. Brett's never been known to take an interest in any woman other than you, as far as I know. He doesn't come across as an importunate lover.'

Sophie gave in to temptation. 'On the contrary,' she said casually. 'Last night he asked me to marry him instead of moving away.'

Alexander grew very still. 'Really?' he said, in a dangerously silky tone. 'And what was your answer?'

'The picture he painted of our future life together was madly attractive,' said Sophie with regret. 'Nevertheless I found the strength to refuse. As you already know, marriage has no place in my particular scheme of things.'

It was very gratifying to hear Alexander's explosive exhalation of relief.

'Thank God for that. Brett's not the husband for you, Sophie.'

Sophie was in full agreement, but saw no reason to let Alexander know it. 'I'm not in the market for any husband,' she said with emphasis, and opened the car door. 'Goodnight, Alexander.'

He jumped out to walk with her through the garden to her front door. 'It's going to be very strange without you at the office on Monday, Sophie.'

'In a day or two you won't notice I've gone,' she assured him. 'Besides, I start work at the new office the following week. Will it be ready by then?'

'Part of it, at least. We may have to dodge ladders and cans of paint for a while, but we should be able to manage.' Alexander watched while Sophie unlocked the door, then bent swiftly and kissed her hard on the mouth before striding back to the car. Sophie listened for a moment until she heard the car start up, then shut the door slowly before turning to find her father leaning in the kitchen doorway in his dressing-gown, watching her.

'Nice evening, pet?' he asked.

'Very nice indeed.' She smiled at him happily. 'Everyone was so kind; they bought me a lovely jardinière for the cottage. Oh, bother—I left it in Alexander's car.'

'He'll keep it safe.' David Gordon kissed her cheek affectionately. 'I thought perhaps you might be feeling blue after saying your farewells, but I knew Alexander would take care of you.'

'What *would* we do without him?' said Sophie mockingly, then returned her father's kiss and went up to bed, thinking she, for one, might be less preoccupied by constant thoughts of Alexander's lovemaking if he were to absent himself from their lives. Then she spent some looking at her bright-eyed reflection in the mirror, coming to terms with the fact that if Alexander were to go out of her life he'd leave a great big gap no one else would ever be likely to fill.

CHAPTER EIGHT

SOPHIE found her free week less free than she'd hoped. Most of it was spent in showing prospective purchasers round the house, a task she found she disliked. Her urge to live alone was as strong as ever; none the less she felt a pang every time she thought of strangers living in the house where she had grown up. It was a great relief when an offer for it came almost at once from the people she liked best.

'And,' she told Kate Paget afterwards, 'perhaps I can have a break from all this frantic housework now the place doesn't have to be inspection-perfect all day and every day!'

The quick sale meant Sophie could begin her new job in Arlesford with a free heart. She was to remain at home until the wedding, after which she planned to stay with her grandmother until Ilex Cottage was ready, and agreed meekly when her father told her she would be foolish to refuse Alexander's offer of driving her to and from Arlesford each day.

Secretly Sophie enjoyed the daily drive with Alexander, who was keeping nobly to his promise to maintain his distance until the wedding was over. She also found it both satisfying and challenging to work with him to set up the new branch, and quickly made her own impression on the office set aside for her own use. The building which housed the offices was old, with lofty rooms and corniced ceilings and more than enough space for the great leather-topped desk Alexander had run to earth in an antique shop. He brought his famous drawing-board from Deansbury, and a squabbed leather chair from his own study at home, and for the time being the elegant proportions of his sanctum were displayed to full effect, uncluttered at this stage by the samples of bricks and tiles and carpets that crowded every corner of the Deansbury offices. Sophie made the most of the peace and space while she could, knowing very well it was only a matter of time before the place was crammed with the overflow from Deansbury.

It was oddly intimate to work with only Alexander for company, with no Perry or George Huntley, or any of the others constantly in and out of her office with their demands. Sophie enjoyed it to the full, not letting herself think about the day when Alexander felt he could relinquish the Arlesford office into Perry's keeping and retreat to his proper place at the helm in Deansbury.

'You can't refuse to lunch with me here,' said Alexander the first day. 'I see no point in your marching off to the local coffee-shop while I eat a lonely lunch in the bar of the Unicorn.'

Neither did Sophie, who was happier to agree than she had any intention of letting him know. Now they were virtually alone together in the offices, give or take a decorator or two, their relationship had quite definitely embarked on a new phase. Sophie could no longer ignore the fact that she was growing steadily more addicted to Alexander's company. It amazed her to think she had once taken him completely for granted as a family friend, or even just as her boss, that she had never once been troubled by the disturbing feelings she now found intensifying towards him daily. All her life Alexander had merely been there, as much a constant in her life as her father or her brothers. Unless one took into account the very brief attack of hero-worship of Alexander at fourteen or so, which had been largely due to the violent envy of her friends the day Alexander collected her from school in the rather flash car he sported in his college days.

The first really deep emotion she had ever experienced towards Alexander, Sophie realised, had been her compassion for him the day he was jilted so publicly by Delphine Wyndham. From that day on it had somehow never been quite possible to resume the old taken-for-granted relationship with Alexander, mainly because he had emerged from the trauma of his bride's defection a subtly changed man. One who seemed to have woken up overnight to the fact that his efficient, familiar secretary was not only a girl he'd known all her life, but a woman with an attraction he was suddenly aware he reacted to strongly.

'I'm behaving excessively well, don't you agree?' he asked smugly over lunch towards the end of the first week in Arlesford.

Sophie laughed. 'An absolute pillar of rectitude!'

'Then let me take you out somewhere on Saturday as my reward.'

'No dice, Alexander. You said after the wedding. Besides, I'm spending the day with Aunt Kate, shopping for last-minute frivolities.'

Alexander, who was looking his spectacular best in chalk-striped grey flannel, sighed as he gazed at her across one of the small tables in the Unicorn's crowded bar. 'You're really going to keep me to my promise, then?'

Sophie nodded. 'You bet your boots I am!'

He eyed her morosely. 'And no doubt the most I can expect *after* the wedding is an occasional meal together. And if I'm very lucky, perhaps a chaste goodnight kiss.' His eyes kindled. 'How I wish we were strangers, Sophie, with no hordes of relatives to inhibit us.'

'By which I assume you feel hampered by the thought of Dad and Aunt Kate.'

'Not to mention the terrible twins!'

Sophie laughed. 'Imagine how disillusioned they'd be if they thought their hero had dishonourable intentions towards a lady!'

'The point being that the lady in this case is their sister.' Alexander grinned. 'It's not their illusions that worry me, believe me, it's their fists. Both of them would be down on me like a ton of bricks, howling vengeance.'

'Good lord, do you think so?' Sophie was much struck by the idea. 'In that case, perhaps you ought to know they've joined a martial arts club.'

Alexander groaned and put a hand over his eyes. 'Heaven preserve me. Your virtue is safe from me, I promise.'

'How disappointing,' said Sophie lightly. 'Come on. Time to get back to work.'

The day of the wedding was cold and showery, not

that the elements were the only factors to make the
occasion very different from Alexander's ordeal.
This time the ceremony took place in the beautiful
Norman church in Deansbury, with flowers and
candles and a bride who arrived to a triumphant
paean of Bach on the first stroke of noon. The
immediate family and a few close friends were the
only guests present, and Kate looked so radiant that
Sophie had to blink away a tear as she watched her
father kiss his bride with moving tenderness.

Afterwards Alexander had organised a superb,
catered lunch at the Chantry, and after it had been
enjoyed, and the toasts drunk and speeches made,
the happy couple set off for a honeymoon in the
Bahamas. Sophie felt a decidedly sharp pang as the
taxi rolled down the drive with her father and Kate
waving through the window until they were out of
sight. Cecily Wainwright, magnificent in mink coat
and hat, intercepted the look in her granddaughter's
eyes and led her back into the house.

'One always feels flat after a wedding. Drink some
champagne,' she commanded, in her usual bracing
way.

Sophie did as she was told, her eyes drawn to
Alexander, who was laughing as Matthew and Mark
regaled him with a catalogue of their exploits in
Edinburgh. 'I feel as though a chapter in my life has
ended,' she said forlornly. 'Does that sound fanciful,
Gran?'

'Not in the least. Perfectly natural since not only
are you moving out of your childhood home, but
your father's acquired a new woman in his life. Not,'
added Mrs Wainwright on reflection, 'that one could

describe Kate as a *new* woman, exactly.'

'True.' Sophie downed a cheering draught of champagne, then steered her grandmother in the direction of the Vicar before going off to cope with a flurry of leavetaking as the guests began to depart. Even the twins, formal suits exchanged for their usual uniform of denim and leather, were bent on setting off for Edinburgh at once.

'The girls in the flat next door are throwing a party tonight,' said Matthew with anticipation as he kissed Sophie. 'We'll give you a ring at Gran's tomorrow.'

Once guests and caterers had gone, Alexander insisted on making tea himself while the two ladies relaxed in his drawing-room.

Mrs Wainwright looked about her curiously. 'Strange how things turn out. Kate will go on as mistress here after all instead of Delphine.'

'Let's forget about Delphine,' said Sophie flatly.

Mrs Wainwright chuckled. 'You consider Alexander's better off without her, I gather.'

'Someone mention my name?' asked Alexander, returning with the tray. 'Will you pour, Mrs Wainwright?'

The elegant old lady was only too happy to oblige, then shocked Sophie rigid by telling Alexander how fortunate he was to be rid of Delphine Wyndham. 'Stupid girl,' she added forcefully. 'Bad-mannered, too. Not done to make a laughing-stock of a fine man like you.'

Sophie glared at her grandparent, appalled. 'For heaven's sake, Gran!'

Alexander looked unruffled. 'I agree, totally. Now Sophie, here, would never dream of behaving like that, would you, Sophie?'

'Few people would!'

'Are you coming back with me in the Bentley, Sophie?' asked Mrs Wainwright, gathering up her gloves.

'She has a long-standing appointment with me tonight,' said Alexander, before Sophie could say a word. 'You haven't forgotten, Sophie, surely?' His eyes gleamed through his thick lashes. 'We arranged it some time ago.'

After the wedding, thought Sophie, taken aback to find Alexander meant it quite so literally.

'Splendid,' said Mrs Wainwright, rummaging in her alligator handbag. 'Here's a key, Sophie. If you're late, let yourself in. I'll probably be in bed. Weddings are so tiring at my age.'

Sophie went with Alexander to install Mrs Wainwright behind the wheel of the ancient Bentley she insisted driving in preference to the modern replacements David Gordon had tried to persuade her to buy over the years. In Cecily Wainwright's opinion the Bentley had more style, and the dignified vehicle continued to delight the inhabitants of Arlesford whenever Mrs Wainwright took to the road.

'Please drive carefully, Gran,' said Sophie anxiously.

'I always do.' Mrs Wainwright gave Alexander a smile. 'Bring her home safely, Alexander.'

Sophie had had quite enough of watching cars roll away from her by this time, and went back into the house with Alexander, feeling even more depressed.

'Will I do as I am?' she asked. 'Since you forgot to

mention any plans for this evening, I haven't brought a change of clothes.'

Because Dr Gordon had provided his daughter with a generous sum to spend on an outfit for the wedding, she had succumbed to the temptation of cashmere the colour of milk chocolate, the thigh-length tunic and brief straight skirt severely plain, unadorned by anything except the wide tortoiseshell bracelet on Sophie's wrist.

'Oh, you'll do,' Alexander informed her, after a long, leisurely survey of her person. 'But I'd like a minute or two to change, if you'll bear with me.'

'Of course.' Sophie took the tea-tray off to the kitchen, feeling ridiculously shy, to her annoyance, glad of a mundane chore like washing cups.

Alexander was back very quickly, his pin-striped Valentino suit replaced by heavy black jersey trousers, and zippered wool jacket over a white wool shirt.

'Right, then, Sophie. Let's go,' he said briskly.

'Where?'

'On a picnic.'

Sophie stared at him in amazement as he hurried her out of the house to the car. 'You've noticed it's almost dark, I suppose,' she said, as she slid inside. '*And* chilly!'

Alexander looked smug. 'I have. But it won't affect the picnic, I promise. Be fair. You *said* I could take you out occasionally for a meal. You didn't specify where.'

Sophie giggled suddenly, her spirits rising as they left Deansbury behind. 'A picnic will certainly be a change from Enzio's!'

'Julian's favourite restaurateur, I assume,' said Alexander scathingly. 'Where the socialites of Deansbury go to see and be seen. Nothing like that tonight, sweetheart. Just you and me.'

A tremor ran up Sophie's spine at the prospect, and Alexander, attuned to it instantly, placed a long-fingered hand on her knee. 'My sole aim is to cheer you up, little sister, I promise, because I could tell the blues were threatening a bit when your father went off with Kate.'

Sophie sighed. 'Yes. Human nature's very strange, isn't it? I've been yearning for my freedom for so long, and now I've been handed it on a plate, so to speak, I don't know quite what to do with it.'

'You'll soon adjust,' he assured her, and began to talk about the wedding.

It was some time before Sophie could pluck up the courage to ask the question which had been niggling at her all day. 'Alexander—was it all very painful for you today?'

Alexander drove in silence for a while. 'To be honest,' he said slowly, 'I did have cold feet about it beforehand. Quite unnecessarily, as it happened. The quiet, moving ceremony we witnessed in church today seemed to have nothing at all to do with my celebrated fiasco.'

'I was worried for you,' she said quietly.

'Thank you.' Alexander hesitated for a moment, glancing at her. 'But it was having you with me that made all the difference, Sophie. I wonder if you can understand that, already, the time with Delphine seems unreal to me, a kind of "brief gaudy hour", when a meteor hurtled into my life for a while, then out of it again. While you, Sophie, have always been there—glowing steadily; the lode-star every man needs in his life.'

Sophie took so much time to digest this that she failed to notice where they were until he halted the car. She peered up at him, eyebrows raised.

'Willow Reach, Alexander? Don't tell me, let me guess. We're having a barbecue in the garden!'

'God, no!' He laughed and left the car to open the big double gates before driving through.

To Sophie's surprise the lights were on in the house. 'Is someone here?'

'No.' He dangled a bunch of keys in front of her nose. 'Willow Reach is now mine, all mine. And the lights are on time switches, of course. You, Miss Gordon, are my very first visitor, but your picnic supper doesn't come cheap—you'll have to work for it.'

'Oh, will I?' Sophie followed Alexander as he unlocked the door and flung it wide before swinging her up in his arms and carrying her though into a large, square hall.

'What *are* you doing?' she said, her face scarlet as he set her on her feet.

He shrugged. 'It just seemed appropriate—all the talk of weddings, I suppose.'

'Then stop talking about them and show me round your house instead,' she said tartly.

Alexander was only too pleased to do so, his manner very proprietorial as he led her upstairs, through empty, beautifully proportioned rooms, fewer in number than Sophie had expected from the size of the house.

'When I originally designed it I made light and space my priorities, rather than room-count.' Alexander gestured towards the windows. 'Great sheets of glass would have been entirely wrong for the garden they looked out on, so I used small panes to create a more cottage-like atmosphere.'

'It's perfect,' said Sophie simply, and ran a hand down the mahogany rail which curved over wrought-iron banisters of such intricate workmanship that they could have been made of fine black lace. She followed Alexander downstairs, through an elegantly fitted kitchen, a sizeable dining-room, a graceful drawing-room with beamed ceiling and shelved alcoves flanking a white marble fireplace. Finally they arrived at the door of a room Alexander announced would be his study.

Sophie's eyes widened as he ushered her inside. Unlike the rest of the rooms, it was anything but empty. Piles of carpet samples were strewn about next to swatches of curtain materials, rolled rugs piled in one corner, canvases stacked in another, and brochures everywhere, for everything from light-fittings to bathrooms and colour-cards for paint. A kilim rug made an oasis in the centre of the floor, and on it stood the only item of furniture Sophie had seen so far in the entire house, a rattan chaise-longue with brown velvet cushions. She grinned at Alexander, enlightened.

'I see, I see. *This* is where we picnic. But before I'm fed I suppose my opinion is required on this lot!'

'Bullseye!' Alexander shrugged off his jacket, then left Sophie alone to browse among all the fabrics, and wonder about the quantity involved for the floors and windows of this tranquil, graceful house.

Alexander returned quickly with a bottle of champagne and two glasses. 'I've had this chilling to the exact degree of perfection in anticipation of this very moment, Miss Gordon.'

Sophie kicked off her shoes and curled up on the chaise-longue with several swatches of curtain material around her, and held out her hand for the glass Alexander was offering. 'Pink champagne, no less,' she said appreciatively. 'To Willow Reach, Alexander; may you be very happy here.'

'Amen to that.' He drank deeply. 'Do you like the house?' he added casually.

'Who wouldn't? If a client ever needs proof of your flair, this house is a wonderful showpiece. Even inside, it just doesn't seem like a modern house. There's a timeless feel to it, as though it's always been here.'

'Probably because so much of the building material was salvaged, as I said when I showed you the garden, from the original house.' Alexander let himself down to sit cross-legged on the rug, then leaned over and refilled her glass. 'Willow Reach was built first time round to house the mistress of one of Charles the Second's courtiers. The gentleman's wife was rich and ugly and very jealous, so he built this house for his beautiful young mistress miles from anywhere, as it was then, with high walls instead of the present hedges, but the same fountain in the grotto in the garden. A secret place where he could be alone with his love, hidden from the world.' Alexander's expressive voice dropped at the last words, as he looked into Sophie's eyes. 'What are you thinking?'

'I was wondering what the girl did with herself while her lover was away at court. All those minutes and hours and days to be filled without him. How on earth did she pass the time?'

'Looking after her children, I imagine,' said Alexander prosaically. 'They produced quite a few, though oddly enough the gentleman was never blessed with a legal heir.'

'Poor rich, ugly wife,' said Sophie with compassion. 'Anyway, Mr Paget, sir, let's get on with the matter in hand.' She shook off the shadow from the past and knelt with Alexander on the floor, quickly engrossed in the colours and textures spread out all around them. His professional eye and her own natural flair for colour worked well together, and the time passed swiftly as they isolated a growing pile of possible choices. Two hours passed before a sudden rumble in Sophie's stomach reminded her it was a long time since the elegant wedding-breakfast at the Chantry.

'I'm hungry,' she said. 'Where's this picnic you promised me, slavedriver?'

Alexander sprang to his feet in remorse. 'Lord, I'm sorry, Sophie. Just stay where you are and I'll bring everything in.'

'Can't I help?'

'No. You've done enough today. Shan't be long.'

Alone, Sophie tidied her hair and stretched out luxuriously on the chaise, thinking about the girl who had lived and loved in the original Willow Reach. What was it like to be someone's mistress? she wondered. Surely a mistress never ironed shirts or cooked

nourishing meals, or even knew how to thread a
needle, let alone sew on all those endless name tapes?
She rather fancied being Alexander's mistress. Her
eyes narrowed as she pictured herself in expensive silk
underwear, with hand-made lace, of course, and a
satin peignoir falling open as she lolled on a chaise-
longue like this, waiting for him to spend long nights
of illicit passion with her, with never a hint of
domestic chores to intrude on their bliss. Her eyes
glittered darkly as she conjured up visions of
weekends in Paris and Rome, holidays in Antigua
and Bali . . .

'That's a very strange look in your eyes, Sophie!'

Sophie came to with a jolt as Alexander came back
with a picnic hamper. She sat up hurriedly, smooth-
ing her brief skirt into place, her cheeks hot.

'Daydreaming,' she said, and helped him set out
their supper on the starched white cloth included in
the hamper. Sophie fell to with a will on the delicious
food provided by Alexander's caterers, with more
appetite now for the slices of pink ham and succulent
turkey breast, the smoked salmon and game pie, than
she had felt for the wedding-breakfast earlier.

'Only cheese to follow, I'm afraid,' said
Alexander. 'I told them to keep it simple, since it had
to hang about for a bit.'

'It's wonderful,' said Sophie indistinctly. 'I'm
starving. Probably because I wasn't in the least
hungry lunch time.'

'I noticed.' Alexander put another slice of ham on
her plate.

They made large inroads on the food, and afterwards finished off the champagne. 'Feel better now?'

asked Alexander lazily. He leaned back against the
foot of the chaise-longue, his legs stretched out in
front of him. Sophie lay on the velvet cushions, a
little drowsy after the good food.

'I certainly do.' She sighed. 'This is such a lovely
house, Alexander. You're a genius.'

'I know,' he said modestly. 'My picnic wasn't a
bad idea, was it?'

'Inspired.' Reluctantly Sophie swung her legs to
the ground and looked around for her shoes. 'Only
now I'm afraid I'll have to ask you to drive me to
Arlesford. I don't want to worry Gran by staying out
late on my first night as her lodger.'

Alexander looked up into her eyes. 'May I have
one kiss first? If you think back, I'm sure we decided
a kiss now and then was acceptable.'

'*You* decided.'

He smiled, and drew her down gently into his arms
and Sophie lay against him, her mouth parting
beneath his so willingly that he crushed her to him
with a groan, kissing her with a hunger she realised
had been kept on a short rein all evening. Then, as
abruptly as it had begun, the storm was over. His
head lifted a little and his embrace relaxed as
gleaming green eyes gazed down into heavy,
slumbering dark ones. 'Does that count as one kiss?'
he muttered against her mouth.

'I wasn't counting,' she whispered.

He drew in a long, shaky breath, then leapt to his
feet, pulling her with him. 'Home!' he said firmly.

CHAPTER NINE

ON A cold November evening a few weeks later, Sophie thrust her paintbrush in a jar of white spirit and eased her aching back as she opened the door to the stairs.

'Coffee, Alexander?' she called.

'Five minutes,' he yelled back. 'Just giving the bedroom ceiling another coat.'

Ilex Cottage was very nearly ready for occupation. Sophie filled her new kettle in her minuscule kitchen, and took a deep breath of satisfaction, coughing a little as the paint fumes hit her chest. Cecily Wainwright had been keen to employ a professional decorator, but Sophie wouldn't hear of it, insisting the little house would be so much more her own if she did the painting herself. And the moment her grandmother learned who was giving a helping hand she said no more.

Alexander eased himself gingerly through the door at the bottom of the stairs, grinning when he saw Sophie sitting cross-legged in the middle of her uncarpeted floor with two mugs of coffee beside her.

'I'm trying not to brush against any of the paintwork,' she said, offering him a packet of biscuits.

Alexander let himself down beside her, flicking a finger at her nose. 'Paint-splash, Sophie.'

She eyed him critically. 'You should see yourself!'

Neither of them were acmes of elegance. Sophie was arrayed in dungarees and sweatshirt, with a peaked denim cap covering her hair, and Alexander wore a black running vest and tracksuit trousers, both garments liberally streaked with white paint.

'What a way to spend Saturday night!' commented Alexander as he munched hungrily.

'I need tomorrow for drying out. Then I can move in on Monday.' Sophie looked about her in triumph. 'All done! Isn't it perfect?'

'You're like a little girl with a doll's house.'

'I never had one, so probably that's why I'm so thrilled with this.' She drank her coffee, her eyes moving in all directions as she arranged furniture in her mind, finally focusing on Alexander, who was watching her with indulgence. She smiled sheepishly. 'Oh, I know it's a bit different from Willow Reach—the entire cottage would probably fit into your drawing-room. But to me this place is everything I've ever wanted.'

Alexander got to his feet and stretched, yawning as he looked at his watch. 'Come on, it's almost midnight. High time you were back at Greenacre.'

Sophie scrambled up, collecting the mugs. She looked over her shoulder at him as he followed her into the kitchen. 'I'm very grateful to you, Alexander. You've been so kind to me lately.'

He removed her paint-stained cap and slid his arms round her from behind, resting his chin on the top of her tousled head.

'Not only kind. Or haven't you noticed? I have also been quite remarkably virtuous and self-restrained, too.'

Sophie slid out of his hold, her eyes dancing as she turned to face him. 'I though maybe the paint was having an effect on your libido!'

He yanked her to him and kissed her, then shook her ungently. 'Don't push your luck, Miss Gordon. My libido happens to be alive and well, since you mention it. I'm merely biding my time.'

She sobered. 'Until when? And for what, exactly?'

Alexander's lashes veiled his expression. 'You'll know when the time comes.'

'Don't be infuriating—tell me!'

'No chance.'

Sophie felt it best to avoid anticipating his intentions a second time. She had been caught like that before, and only by the grace of God managed to avoid refusing a proposal of marriage Alexander had never intended making. This time, she could only think he must be waiting for her to move out from under her grandmother's roof before finally asking to share her bed.

It was a thought which preoccupied her a great deal over the next few days, all the time she was settling in to her new home and helping her grandmother make the transition from Greenacre to the suite of rooms she was to occupy at Broad Oaks. Mrs Wainwright had insisted on overseeing the packing of her possessions, most of which she had been adamant over putting into storage for future use by Sophie and her brothers, and when the upheaval was finally over and the indomitable lady was at last installed in her new quarters Sophie was worried to see how tired her grandmother looked. She said so afterwards in no uncertain terms to her father and Kate, who had joined in the supervision of the move.

David Gordon exchanged a glance with Kate, then suggested all of them go to Ilex Cottage to see the finished result. When an admiring tour of inspection had been made the three of them sat with glasses of the sherry provided by Perry as a 'libation to the god of removals', and Dr Gordon explained to Sophie that Cecily Wainwright's heart was not as strong as it might be.

'When I heard she was moving herself into Broad Oaks I had a talk with her—behind your back, pet, I'm afraid.' He squeezed Sophie's hand reassuringly. 'Don't look like that! She'll last for years yet, as long as she takes it easy, with a regular professional eye kept on her. Your grandmother's a very sensible woman, and she's done the best possible thing under the circumstances.'

'I had no idea,' said Sophie with remorse. 'She never said a word.'

'And she won't thank your father for letting the cat out of the bag,' said Kate gently. 'So keep it to yourself, Sophie. Just go on as usual.' She grinned. 'You know how incensed she'd be if she thought David had spilled the beans.'

'Lord, yes!' Sophie smiled ruefully, and changed the subject by asking how they liked her colour-scheme. Kate was loud with her approval of the yellow and white curtains, and how well the dining-room carpet from Greenacre had cut down to suit the small room.

'I love the chaise-longue, too,' she added. 'Was that Cecily's?'

'No. Alexander donated it as a moving-in present,' said Sophie casually. 'Perfect there, isn't it?'

Except for the disquieting news about her grandmother, life was good for Sophie in the period following her move to Ilex Cottage. She saw less of Alexander, it was true, because Perry was now in charge of the Arlesford branch of Paget's. Nevertheless, in his role of senior partner Alexander visited the branch office fairly often, and followed his original plan of taking Sophie out for an occasional meal, or a trip to the theatre in Bath or Bristol, but he firmly refused her offers of a meal at Ilex Cottage by way of return.

'No, Sophie,' he said one night, as he saw her safely into the cottage. 'I'm giving you the breathing space you wanted, behaving like the virtuous family friend I'm believed to be. But frankly I don't think my virtue is so absolute as to survive an evening *à deux* with you, my lovely, neither here nor at Willow Reach.'

Sophie switched on a lamp then sat on the chaise, looking up at him in challenge. 'What if I don't *want* it to survive, Alexander?'

His mouth tightened as he gazed down at her. The soft cashmere of the suit she'd worn for the wedding outlned the curves of her breasts as Sophie clasped her hands deliberately behind her head, and crossed her legs in their gossamer dark stockings so that her skirt rode high above her knees.

'Sophie——' He stopped, running a hand through his hair as he flung away to the fireplace.

'Really, Alexander! I'm no Victorian maiden, likely to faint if you catch a glimpse of my ankles.'

'I can see a lot more than that!' He kept his back turned. 'I'm sure you've been told how beautiful your legs are hundreds of times, so just pull your skirt down and behave, Sophie.'

She sat up straight, addressing his broad shoulders. 'Perhaps I was wrong. Yet I could have sworn you'd changed towards me, Alexander. Lately you've been giving me the impression that you think of me as a bit more than just Sophie the family friend, or even Sophie the secretary. *Was* I wrong, Alexander?'

He swung round, his eyes glittering. He stared down at her for a moment, then caught her hands and hauled her up against him. 'You know damn well you weren't wrong.' He moved her hand to touch him. 'Does *that* feel as though I don't want you? Why the hell do you think I keep inventing reasons to interfere at the Arlesford office? Just to see you, my little friend! Perry gets bloody fed up with me, only he knows very well it's your neck I want to breathe down, not his.'

Sophie moved her hand delicately, exulting in his anguished groan as he crushed her to him and began to kiss her with all the urgency she'd been yearning for over the past weeks of impersonal friendliness. She'd been frantic for his touch, eager to breathe in the distinctive scent of him, feel the warmth of his body against hers. Her nerves were ragged with wanting him, and after a long, breath-less interval Sophie tipped her head back, her eyes dilated as she gazed up into his.

'Take me to bed, Alexander,' she whispered, triumphantly certain he'd sweep her up into his arms. Instead his arms fell away and he shook his head, his eyes tight closed.

'No?' she said incredulously.

'I *can't*, Sophie!' The words were bitten out.

'Oh, God, not you as well!' Sophie turned away, hugging her arms across her chest.

'What the hell do you mean by that?' Alexander caught her by the elbow and spun her round. 'How many men do you ask to take you to bed, may I ask?'

'Only you, Alexander, only you.' Sophie's eyes flashed at him, humiliation and anger vibrating inside her. 'But don't worry. I won't again. Ever!'

He shook her hard. 'Listen to me, you little shrew. When you moved in here I had several requests from a number of people. Not couched in similar terms precisely, but all amounting to the same thing. Your grandmother, your father, Kate too; they all asked me to keep an eye on you, to take care of you, see you were all right on your own. Now maybe they intended me to check your pipes didn't freeze, or your drains didn't block. It's possible. But you know and I know that they meant me to see that no man gets ideas because little Sophie's living alone now. And I think they include me, Sophie, since I think I can safely say I *am* a man.'

She pulled free. 'Not merely a man, Alexander—

a paragon of perfection.' She put her hands behind her back, her eyebrows raised. 'Why not come clean? Admit I don't compare with Delphine in the sex department.'

Alexander gritted his teeth. 'For God's sake, what do I have to do to convince you I don't care a damn for Delphine any more?'

'Take me to bed and make love to me!' She eyed him defiantly. 'Why not? You've been here with me on several occasions lately, long enough to make love to me every time. Who's to know you haven't? Probably all the neighbours think we're lovers, anyway.'

'But we're not! And your family trusts me to see that we stay that way.'

'Then I think we'd better revert to our original relationship in future. Employer and employee.' Sophie quivered inside with wounded pride and something she assumed was sexual frustration. It was a new feeling. One that humiliated and hurt and spurred her on to lash out, to puncture Alexander's armour of rectitude.

'Our original relationship was also friendship,' he reminded her coldly.

'Then let's decide on a new relationship, with no personal feelings involved.' She went to the door. 'Thank you for dinner, Alexander. I won't say the evening was an unqualified success—but thank you just the same.'

'Does this mean I see you only at the office?' He stood over her, his eyes shuttered in his pale face. 'Can't we at least be friends?'

'I've had it up to here with men who just want to

be friends. It's very bad for a girl's self-esteem. Goodnight, Alexander.' Sophie opened the door, waiting pointedly. He gazed at her for a moment, then grabbed her by the shoulders and kissed her savagely.

'A pity to disappoint the neighbours,' he flung at her, then strode off down the narrow walk, leaving Sophie a prey to seething emotions as she banged the door shut and stormed upstairs to bed.

'Bad night?' asked Perry next day, as Sophie finished going through the post with him.

'No,' she snapped, then smiled apologetically. 'Sorry. Didn't mean to bite.'

'Don't mention it—just don't like to see you down in the mouth.' Perry eyed her closely. 'Weren't you dining with my cousin and revered boss last night?'

'Yes.' Sophie got up. 'Shall I make coffee now?'

'In other words mind your own business, E.P. Paget, Junior Partner.' He grinned, his blue eyes alight with curiosity. 'Don't tell me Alexander came on a bit strong, Sophie! Shall Uncle Perry slap his wrist for you?'

Sophie gave him a withering look and marched back to her office without deigning to reply. Her depression was acute. Her satisfaction over giving Alexander his marching orders had lasted less than the time taken to get herself to bed, leaving her utterly miserable, and prone to looking up hopefully every time her office door opened next day. But it was always Perry, or Brian Harris the young draughtsman, never Alexander. Each ring of the telephone had her diving for the receiver, but it was never the desired voice on the other end of the line. To her dismay even her delight in her new home was dimmed by her quarrel with Alexander, and as the days went by her evenings alone in the cottage began to feel lonely instead of peaceful. The rest of the week passed without contact with Alexander of any kind, professional or otherwise, so that Sophie was only too glad to accept an invitation to Sunday lunch with her father and Kate. She was helping the latter in the kitchen when she heard Alexander's voice in the hall. Kate's eyebrows rose as she saw Sophie stiffen.

'Didn't I mention Alexander was coming, love?'

'No, you didn't. How nice.'

It was not at all nice. The meal was an ordeal, since Alexander's manner towards Sophie was chillingly polite, and her reaction was to chatter nineteen to the dozen to hide her dismay. Kate and David Gordon, plainly worried by the constraint between their respective loved ones, did their best to keep the conversational ball rolling, but it was uphill work.

Sophie was deeply pleased to see Alexander looked haggard, as if lack of sleep was a problem they shared.

'How is Willow Reach?' she asked brightly. 'Everything done now?'

'More or less.' He met her eyes. 'The curtains you chose look exactly right, by the way. They were hung on Friday.'

'Oh, splendid. No—no, thanks, Aunt Kate, no pudding.'

'You haven't eaten much,' observed her father.

'Are you cooking proper meals for yourself these days?'

'Yes, Doctor, I am!' Sophie avoided Alexander's sardonic gaze and began a conversation with Kate on a televised opera they had both watched during the week, and shortly afterwards Alexander rose to go.

'May I give you a lift, Sophie? Arlesford is very little out of my way.'

'No, thanks. I'm staying to tea—if that's all right with you, Aunt Kate?'

Kate agreed with alacrity, and pressed Alexander to stay, but he took his leave with the air of a man desperate to escape.

'You two had a fight?' enquired Dr Gordon, while Kate was seeing her stepson off.

'Yes. Nothing to worry about.' Sophie smiled brightly and went off to help Kate wash up.

Sophie had refused Perry's invitations to lunch at the Unicorn right from the start, but next day he insisted she broke her rule. He was in jubilant mood and wanted to celebrate. Confirmation had just been received that the firm had won the Waterside Hotel job in Brading.

'Clever lad, our Alexander,' said Perry, as he brought their drinks to the table. 'Sorry for the delay, by the way. They're short-staffed.'

Sophie sipped her wine absently, her mind on the last occasion she'd been here. With Alexander.

'What's up, Sophie?' asked Perry affectionately. 'Anyone with half an eye can tell you and Alexander have called a halt to whatever's been going on between you. And,' he added, 'that neither of you is exactly happy about it.'

'There was nothing "going on", as you so delicately put it.' Nor likely to be, thought Sophie unhappily.

'Sorry—rather thought there was, myself.' Perry shrugged. 'I mean you've known each other forever, of course. But since that ghastly business with Delphine I fancy Alexander's a changed man in more ways than one. He fancies you rotten these days, Sophie, old family friend or not.'

'Nonsense,' said Sophie flatly, her heart leaping at the mere thought of being fancied by Alexander.

Perry put out a hand to cover hers. 'And I've seen Willow Reach. I know you helped choose a lot of the stuff there, so naturally I thought——'

'Well, you thought wrong.'

'So you're just good friends?'

'No, Perry.' Sophie swallowed hard, her eyes suddenly misting over. 'We're not even friends any more.'

'So *here* you are!'

Sophie jumped yards as Alexander's voice interrupted them. She stared up at him guiltily, her heart sinking at the look of icy disapproval on his handsome face as he loomed over them.

'We're celebrating,' said Perry, unabashed. 'What'll you have, Alexander?'

'Celebrating?' Alexander's voice grated, and Perry gazed at him, all blue-eyed innocence.

'The Waterside Hotel, of course, old chap.' He smiled benignly and went off to push his way to the bar.

'May I join you?' asked Alexander stiffly.

'Yes. Do.' Sophie swallowed some wine to moisten her suddenly dry mouth. 'Congratulations, by the way. You must be very pleased.'

'Thank you.' Alexander stared down at the table. 'Do you lunch here with Perry every day?'

'No. First time today, in fact. He insisted on celebrating your success.' Sophie looked away across the crowded bar, battling to keep calm.

'Is all well at the cottage?'

'Fine.'

'Good. How's your grandmother?'

'Much better now she's settled in. She's quite spoiled by the staff at Broad Oaks.'

Alexander put a hand out to touch hers. 'Sophie——' He bit back a curse as Perry came back, juggling three glasses.

'I ordered lunch for you with ours, Alexander,' he panted. 'Like a rugger scrum back there. Miranda's left. The blonde behind the bar,' he added, as the other two looked blank.

Sophie picked at her prawn-stuffed crêpe while Perry wolfed his steak sandwich then jumped up, saying he had an appointment. He pushed Sophie down into her seat as she rose to leave with him, telling her to finish her lunch like a good girl, and not to rush back to the office.

Alone together, both Sophie and Alexander gave up all pretence at eating.

'Alexander——'

'Sophie——'

They spoke together, then stopped short, looking at each other, and Alexander smiled for the first time.

'I can't stand it, Sophie. I've been bloody miserable since that night. Too much time to think in my empty house.'

'I've thought a lot, too,' said Sophie.

'Were any of the thoughts about me?' He took her hand in his under the table, stroking it with his fingers.

'Of course they were. Why were you so cold and distant to me yesterday?' she blurted.

'*I* was cold and distant? Good God—*you* were the original Snow Queen. One look from you and I had icicles on my roast beef!'

Sophie gave a choked laugh, then sobered as she found him looking at her with such intensity she gazed back wordlessly, as the pupils of his thickly fringed eyes dilated, holding her in thrall.

'I miss you, Sophie,' he said softly. 'All I can think of are those words you said.'

'Which words?'

'The request you made, my darling. If you could bring yourself to repeat it, I'd respond differently this time, I promise. I've decided I can't spend my life trying to please everyone but you and me.' He leaned closer, his hand tightening on hers. 'Ask me again, Sophie.'

'Here?'

'Yes. Here. And now.'

Sophie couldn't tear her eyes away from his. The noise and laughter all around them faded into nothingness. All she could see was Alexander and the hypnotic urgency of his gaze as he willed her to say what he wanted. She shivered, and his hand tightened on hers as she ran the tip of her tongue over suddenly dry lips. 'If I remember correctly,' she whispered, 'I said——'

'*Alexander!*' cried a high, fluting voice, shattering the spell. 'What a chase I've had, darling! I popped into your old office first, then I simply roared over here in Daddy's Jag to this new place, and some Brian person told me I'd find you in the pub. And here you are!' Delphine Wyndham stood over them, a fur coat slung over a gold jumpsuit. She turned the full force of her celebrated smile on the two people staring at her in frozen silence, her eyes narrowing as she looked from one rigid face to the other.

Sophie felt as though she were living through a bad dream as Alexander rose slowly to his feet, his face a handsome mask.

'Hello, Delphine,' he said quietly. 'Quite a surprise.'

'I'm back, darling,' Delphine announced blithely, the smile blinding as a ripple of intense interest ran through the entire bar. She preened, visibly lapping up the attention she was attracting, then turned to Sophie, who felt suddenly helpless, like a mouse transfixed by the predatory gaze of a sleek, black cat. 'He*llo,* Sophie—lovely to see you again. Still slaving away for Alexander, then?'

At which Sophie came to life and rose to her feet, gathering up her bag and scarf. She gave Delphine a composed little smile. 'Hello, Delphine. I'm sure you won't think me rude if I dash. Mustn't keep my boss waiting. I work for Perry in the branch office here these days.' She aimed the smile at Alexander's chin. 'Goodbye.'

'Sophie——' he said urgently, catching her arm as she passed, but she detached herself and began to push her way through the crowd.

''Bye, Sophie,' called Delphine, and laid a possessive hand on Alexander's arm. 'Now then, darling. Aren't you going to buy me a drink?'

Sophie fled blindly, bumping into Anna Mitchell, the wife of the proprietor.

'Sorry,' panted the latter. 'Utter chaos here today. God knows what we'll do tonight.'

'Do you need help in the bar?' asked Sophie urgently.

'Do we! Know anyone who could fill in for a night or two?'

'Yes. Me.'

CHAPTER TEN

SOPHIE'S offer, made on the spur of the moment, was a gut reaction to the shock of seeing Delphine. Brushing aside Anna Mitchell's thanks, she hurried away from the Unicorn, blind to everything but the expression on Alexander's face as he looked up to find Delphine smiling at him. He had stared at that exquisite face like a man in a dream, thought Sophie in misery. For herself the whole thing had been a nightmare, a brutal interruption of a moment which just possibly might have marked a turning point in her life.

The afternoon which followed was an experience Sophie hoped never to repeat. She spent it on tenterhooks, half hoping, half dreading Alexander might appear at any moment, Delphine in tow. All Sophie wanted was to be put out of her misery one way or another, but she was left in what could be loosely termed as peace. Perry never returned to the office after dashing off on a house inspection, and Brian Harris and his minions were deep in piles of drawings and prints for a new factory. It seemed an eternity before Sophie was free to go home at last, on fire with the desire to scrub herself from head to foot, feeling somehow that hot water and soap might wash away the humiliation of almost begging Alexander to be her lover, when he

obviously still hankered after his Delphine. She
could have kicked herself. Making a fool of oneself
once was allowable. Twice was lunacy. Sophie
sluiced water over her hair and face, mortified that
she could actually have forgotten how beautiful
Delphine really was. What man could look at such
perfection without wanting to possess it? And
Alexander, if he were to be believed, had never
actually been granted the privilege. Which made it
all so much worse. Men always, as Alexander had
once informed her, wanted most the things they
were refused. While she, thought Sophie,
shuddering, had actually offered herself to him
twice. *Twice*!

Sophie attacked her hair with dryer and
hairbrush, then made a sandwich and crumbled it
to pieces while she drank cup after cup of strong
black coffee, pacing up and down her little sitting-
room until it was time to set off for the Unicorn.

Monday evenings, Anna Mitchell informed her,
were quieter than the rest of the week. Sophie was
grateful for it since it gave her the chance to
memorise prices, learn how to pull pints of beer
and handle the optics, to wash and replace glasses,
and generally accustom herself to the routine of the
job. Frank Mitchell, the landlord, was a stalwart
man with a pleasant but authoritative manner,
popular with his clientèle. Sophie found him easy
to work with from the start, mainly because she
learned rapidly, and was quick on her feet. One
thing he found hard to tolerate, Frank told her
bluntly, was a barmaid who dawdled or spent too
much time chatting up the younger male

customers. Sophie was astonished anyone ever had time for chat with anyone from behind the bar of the Unicorn, and went home at closing time feeling very tired indeed. She could hear the telephone ringing as she unlocked her door and burst into the sitting-room just as it stopped. She glared at the telephone in frustration, sure it had been Alexander. She scowled. If he really wanted to talk to her he would ring again. She went upstairs and dawdled as long as possible while she undressed, then lay in tense expectancy, sure the telephone would ring again. It was only when it became obvious at last that it was going to do no such thing that she gave in at last and let herself cry her misery into her pillow.

Perry was waiting when Sophie arrived at the office next day.

'Morning, Sophie.' He handed her a note. 'I was ordered to give you this before we start.'

Sophie thanked him, her mouth tightening as she saw Alexander's familiar handwriting.

'I rang last night—repeatedly—without success. I'm in court all day today, but I'll be at the cottage tonight about eight. A.'

Sophie screwed the paper into a ball and threw it in the wastebasket without comment, then applied herself to the usual matters of the day, knowing quite well that Perry was bursting with curiosity. She made no attempt to satisfy it, and the morning's post was dealt with and Sophie almost out of his office before Perry succumbed to temptation.

'Delphine's back, I hear,' he said, opening the

door for Sophie.

'Yes. You should have stayed yesterday.' She gave him a mocking little smile. 'You missed all the fun.'

Perry looked concerned. 'Look, love, I'm sure Alexander——'

'It's all right,' Sophie interrupted gently. 'Really, it is. Now I must get on.'

There was more to do than usual, to Sophie's eternal gratitude. She relegated Alexander's note to the back of her mind, refusing to lose her temper over the autocratic tone of his message. But as she took a break for lunch she allowed herself a small glow of triumph at a mental picture of Alexander knocking in vain on the door of her empty cottage later. If he wanted to see her, he'd have to find her first.

Sophie ran into Sam Jefford on her way to a snack lunch at the coffee-shop, and instead of avoiding her like the plague, as he had done on various occasions beforehand in the town, he stopped to speak to her.

'I hope you're settling in happily in Ilex Cottage, Sophie,' he said, smiling diffidently.

Sophie assured him she was, and fell into step with him as they walked along.

'Have you forgiven me?' he asked.

She laughed. 'If you mean about the job, of course I have.'

'I really felt very bad about letting you down, you know.'

Sophie felt touched. 'As it happened, it all turned out very well in the end, so please don't be embarrassed about it.'

Sam's face relaxed as he asked if he could buy Sophie lunch at the Unicorn by way of amends.

'No! I mean, no, thank you.' Sophie smiled brightly. 'I'm helping out there in the evenings for a while until they get someone permanent, so I'd rather steer clear in the daytime.'

When Sam suggested the coffee-shop instead it seemed churlish to refuse, and Sophie spent a pleasant interlude with him, her raw wounds soothed just a little by his rather touching efforts to please. Consequently she was late back at the offices, which were empty, except for a very unexpected visitor. Delphine Wyndham was enthroned behind the desk in Sophie's office, her gold eyes alight with malicious glee at the look on Sophie's face.

'Hello, Sophie,' she said, and got up, stretching as she pushed back the chair. She looked spectacular in the type of clinging, draped dress only the very slender could wear, with yesterday's fur coat suspended negligently from one shoulder, and, most eye-catching of all, the emerald engagement ring Alexander had given her prominent on her left hand.

'I happened to be passing, so I thought I'd pop in for a chat.' Delphine ran her left hand over her hair.

Just in case I'd missed the ring, thought Sophie. 'How nice,' she said coolly. 'May I offer you tea, or coffee?'

'No, darling, can't stay. I just came to put you in the picture, so to speak. Regarding our mutual friend.'

'You're a Dickens fan?' asked Sophie in mock surprise.

'What *are* you talking about?' Delphine sauntered to the door, then turned, lounging gracefully in the opening. 'OK Sophie. Let's get things straight. I'm back now. For good. So Alexander won't be in need of anything *you* have to offer, if I make myself plain.'

Sophie seated herself behind the desk, regarding her visitor with a serenity designed to hide the murder she felt in her heart.

'What a bitch you are, Delphine,' she said conversationally. 'I assume the LA contract fell through—or did Terry Foyle find a younger face for the Americans? After all, as models go, you're getting on a bit, aren't you?'

Delphine's face convulsed with a rage that obliterated its beauty. She leaned her hands on the desk and glared at Sophie. 'Little cow! How *dare* you? I know you've been dangling after Alexander all these years, but you can forget all that, Goody Two-Shoes. Delphine's back, and she's everything Alexander Paget ever wanted. And I do mean *wanted*. You, darling, just can't compete!'

Sophie shrugged. 'Don't panic, Delphine. You won't get any competition from me. A husband is not on my list of requirements. Run away and play with Alexander to your heart's content.' She looked at her watch pointedly, and drew a file towards her. 'Now, if you don't mind I have a lot to get through. I have a date tonight, and I'm rather keen to leave on time for once.'

Delphine backed away, disconcerted. 'Yes—well, as long as you know how things stand.' She drew the opulent fur around her, eyeing Sophie suspiciously. 'Who was the man with you outside?'

'Sam Jefford. Estate agent.'

'Did you have lunch with him?'

Sophie nodded, resigned. 'Yes.'

'Is he your date tonight?'

Sophie shuffled her papers pointedly. 'Not that it's any business of yours, but no, he isn't.'

Delphine shook her head blankly. 'I can't see what men see in you. I mean, you're not exactly a raving beauty, are you?'

'Perhaps it's the beauty of my nature which appeals. Now goodbye, Delphine.' Sophie turned away to her typewriter, wincing at the bang of the door as her visitor finally departed.

Sophie's mood was evil for the rest of the afternoon, half her mind on autopilot as she worked, the other half reviling Alexander Paget and Delphine Wyndham with impartial violence.

Stung by Delphine's insults, Sophie took great care with her appearance that night before setting off for the Unicorn. To bolster her much-tried ego she put on a black knitted dress livened up by a choker of giant silver and black beads, and was glad she'd taken the trouble when Frank Mitchell winked appreciatively at the sight of her.

'Very nice, Sophie. Just the thing to attract the punters.'

He was right. Sophie was run off her feet all evening, unlike the night before.

'Is it always like this on Tuesdays?' she gasped at one stage, as she polished glasses furiously.

'Tonight and every night,' Anna assured her. 'Don't knock it, love, it's business. And you're doing really well. Don't fancy giving up the day job and coming here on a permanent basis, by any chance?'

In Sophie's present mood it was a tempting thought. And if only Alexander were involved she knew she might have been rash enough to say yes. But there was Perry to consider, and all the others. And her feet. They would never stand it. She shook her head regretfully, then turned to a group of new arrivals with a smile.

'Good evening, gentlemen. What can I get you?'

Sophie shivered as she walked home. It had been stormy all day, but now the wind was at gale force, and clouds scudded wildly across a moonlit sky as she turned away from the lights of the town to make for Church Row. The wind howled demonically in the trees, funnelling through the narrow walk between churchyard and cottages, with a force that blew Sophie's hair in her eyes and bit icily through her raincoat. In a lull between gusts she halted, stiffening, sure she could hear footsteps. Telling herself she was tired, hearing things, she began to run the last few yards towards the cottage, her heart in her throat as the footsteps behind her quickened in pace with her own. As she reached her front door a hand caught her arm and she screamed as she spun round. Then the moon burst from the clouds to illumine Alexander's unmistakable fair head, and she glared up at him, almost beside herself with rage.

'What the hell do you think you're doing?' she spat.

'Where the *hell* have you been?' he demanded harshly in turn, ignoring her. He took her by the elbows. 'Didn't you get my note?'

Sophie shook him off. 'Oh, yes. I got your note.' She unlocked her door, then turned on him coldly. '*You* were the one who said you'd be here at eight, not me.'

Alexander opened the door and thrust her unceremoniously inside, his eyes glittering dangerously as he banged the door shut, then stood leaning against it, arms folded. 'I rang you at intervals all yesterday evening, until it got so late I assumed you must have gone off to stay with Kate. So I scribbled the note and gave it to Perry before I dashed off to court this morning. I should have taken time to couch it in more flowery terms I assume—beg you to deign to be in tonight. Where *were* you two nights running, for God's sake?'

Sophie shrugged out of her raincoat, her face flushed with anger. 'It's nothing to do with you where I spend my evenings.'

'My mistake. I thought it was.' Colour flared along Alexander's cheekbones, emphasising the white line round his mouth. 'I suppose this—this tantrum is because of Delphine.'

'Tantrum!' Sophie's eyes flamed at him. 'Just go, Alexander. Back to the loving arms of your faithful fiancée.' She spat the word at him, and Alexander came away from the door with a lunge, catching her by the hands.

'You're jealous!' His eyes gleamed with a triumph Sophie found unbearable.

'*Jealous?* Ha!' She tried to break free, but Alexander was ready for her and tightened his grip. 'Will you let me go?' she panted. 'I've had a long day and I'm tired, and I just want you to get out of here.'

'Who is he?' Alexander rapped.

Sophie glared at him. 'Who's who?'

He released one of her hands and brushed his fingers over her breasts with insulting familiarity. 'You're all dressed up for someone.'

Utterly enraged, Sophie dodged away and picked up the poker. 'Get out, Alexander Paget. Get out right now, before I do you an injury, you two-timing swine!'

'Sophie!' Alexander threw his hands wide in despair. 'What's got into you, for God's sake? OK, so Delphine turned up again. Is *that* the reason for all this?'

'Ten out of ten for observation! Now get out!'

'Look here, Sophie Gordon. I've been stuck in a car at the end of your lane for hours, just waiting to see you. I was getting bloody frantic by the time you turned up, and I'm not moving from here until you tell me what's eating you.'

'Then you'll stay here all night!' Too late, Sophie realised what she'd said. She retreated in alarm as Alexander advanced on her, his eyes narrowed to gleaming slits.

'With the greatest of pleasure. Give me that poker.'

'No!' Sophie swung it at him wildly, but

Alexander grabbed it in mid-flight, wrenching it out of her hand. He tossed it in the hearth and jerked her towards him.

'All right,' he said through gritted teeth. 'We'll leave the talking until afterwards.'

Afterwards? Sophie's mouth opened in protest but he closed it summarily with his own. For a split-second she yielded and his hold tightened, then she began to fight in earnest, kicking at him with high, slender heels, wrenching a hand free to grab at his hair, but Alexander was oblivious to it all. The beads broke and rolled in all directions, but he never lifted his mouth from hers, suffocating her protests, impervious to her flailing hands as he lifted her off her feet.

Sophie kicked and struggled like a wild thing, but Alexander merely man-handled her across the room and wrenched open the door to the stairs. Their ascent to the bedroom was violent and undignified, both of them coming into painful contact with the walls as Alexander stumbled inexorably upward, determined to deposit his writhing burden where he intended, on her bed.

The moment Sophie hit the quilt she scrambled up like an eel, but Alexander threw himself after her in a rugby tackle, catching her by the ankles and hauling her back along the bed. The clinging dress rode upward, displaying lace-topped hold-up stockings, and more, at which point Alexander lost whatever shreds of civilisation he had left. He groaned like a man in anguish and pulled her beneath him, his mouth hot on hers as his hand sought the warmth of a satiny thigh above the stocking. Sophie threshed her head back and forth, making choked sounds of protest, but Alexander's response was to straddle her with two muscular legs, one hand on her mouth as he struggled to rid himself of his jacket with the other. Neither of them heard the rising howl of the wind, both of them so locked in primitive sexual combat they were deaf and blind to anything but escape on one hand and mastery on the other. 'Let me go!' screeched Sophie, her voice unrecognisable as he took his hand from her mouth. Alexander's laugh was a deadly little sound, leaving Sophie in no doubt that, whatever he had in mind, freeing her was no part of it. At last he was out of the heavy leather jacket, and he leaned away a little to toss it on the floor. Instantly Sophie seized her chance, desperation lending her strength as she writhed free from his restraining legs and threw herself towards the foot of the bed just as the window blew in with an almighty crash and something hard and sharp connected with Sophie's head.

'Sophie!' Alexander's cry was agonised as he leapt for the light, his feet crunching on broken glass as he turned to see her sitting, dazed, in a heap of broken glass, staring at a bloody tuft of hair and skin lying on the pale yellow quilt. Wind howled through the room from the shattered window, and she lifted blank eyes to Alexander as he carefully cleared the broken glass away from her so he could lift her off the bed.

'Your face is cut,' she remarked.

'Never mind me.' His eyes glittered darkly in his chalk-white face. 'Are you all right, my darling?'

She nodded, then gasped as blood poured down her forehead and on to her hands and all over Alexander's white shirt, and suddenly there was a violent pain in her head and she began to scream as he lifted her in his arms and ran down the stairs at twice the speed of their recent ascent. Afterwards everything was a blur. Sophie was dimly aware through the pain and cold that she was in a car, then in a brightly lit room smelling of antiseptic, and there were nurses and young men in white coats, who took X-rays and gave her injections and did unspeakable things to her scalp with needles and thread and it all hurt unbearably, and then she was sick, and embarrassed and shivering when they cut the black dress off her and it stuck in places where bits of glass had speared her through the wool, leaving deep little cuts the nurses drew together with butterfly dressings, and finally, blessedly, she was tucked into bed and allowed to sleep.

When Sophie woke it was daylight and her father and Kate were standing beside her bed. She smiled gingerly, wincing as pain knifed through her head.

'I'm not going to say "where am I", because I assume I'm in Arlesford General,' she said hoarsely.

'Yes, pet.' Dr Gordon took her hand in his. 'How do you feel?'

'I've got a fair old headache, but I think I'm OK.' Sophie smiled at Kate. 'Sorry to give you a fright, Stepmama.'

Kate let out a deep breath. 'I'll overlook it this time. Don't do it again, please, darling.'

'How's Alexander? Is he all right?'

'A few cuts, otherwise fine.' Dr Gordon gave his
daughter a wry look. 'I'm not sure why he was in
your bedroom when the window blew in, but thank
God he was there. You'd have been in a sorrier
state altogether if that gash in your scalp hadn't
been attended to at once, I assure you.'

Sophie's face turned from white to crimson then
white again, and Kate pulled at her husband's
hand.

'Go on, David. You'll be late for morning
surgery. I'll stay with Sophie.'

'Kate's taking you home to the Chantry once
you've been discharged,' said Dr Gordon briskly.

'Oh, lovely.' Sophie tried to smile. 'My own
doctor in the house if I have a relapse.'

Later in the morning a very shaky Sophie
stumbled into the Chantry with Kate, grateful for
the latter's ministrations as she was installed on a
comfortable couch, and fussed over a little. When
Dr Gordon arrived at lunch time Alexander was
with him, looking pale and exhausted, his cheek
and temple decorated, like Sophie's, with butterfly
plasters. After assuring himself his daughter was all
right, Dr Gordon withdrew to the kitchen with
Kate, leaving Alexander alone with the invalid.

'Is the cottage in a bad way?' asked Sophie,
avoiding Alexander's eyes.

'Perry's checking the damage. I had to be in
court again this morning. Another boundary
dispute.' He sat on the edge of the couch and took
one of her scarred hands in his. 'Are you really all
right, Sophie? I thought they'd have kept you in

hospital longer.'

Sophie smiled. 'Not for a mere crack on the head. It must have been some gale—Casualty had a very busy night.'

'So I gather.'

'How do you like my dressing? Rather chic—like a Sikh topknot, don't you think?'

Alexander leaned nearer. 'Stop chattering and let me apologise. I'm so hellish sorry, Sophie. If I hadn't resorted to caveman tactics it would never have happened.'

Sophie flushed and looked down at her hands. 'Rubbish. If you hadn't been there I'd have been in bed anyway, so I'd still have copped it when the window blew in.'

'The fact remains that if I hadn't hauled you upstairs at that particular juncture you wouldn't have been injured.' His voice was so bitter with self-loathing, Sophie tried to raise his spirits with a mischievous little smile.

'Oh, come on, Alexander. It does have a funny side. I thought the earth was supposed to move, not the sky fall in!'

Alexander's startled look warmed slowly to a smile. 'Does this mean you're not angry with me any more? You were fighting mad last night, and I still don't know why.'

She looked at him hard, but it was quite plain he meant what he said. 'Are you being entirely honest?'

He shrugged. 'It's obvious Delphine's at the bottom of it—God knows, she could hardly have materialised at a less opportune moment.' His eyes met hers very directly. 'But why were you so furious with *me,* Sophie? I had no idea she was back, I promise.'

'No,' agreed Sophie drily. 'I could see that.' She contemplated him thoughtfully for a moment or two, then gave him the details of Delphine's warning-off visit, and watched, fascinated, as Alexander's face, normally so inscrutable, darkened from incredulity to murderous fury by the end of her little tale.

'My God!' he said, seething. 'And you believed her?'

'She was flashing her engagement ring at me, Alexander. Why wouldn't I believe her?' Sophie looked down. 'Besides, I'd forgotten how beautiful she is. So had you, by the look on your face when she turned up in the Unicorn bar.'

Alexander put a hand under her chin and turned her face up to his. 'Sophie, I swear I made it crystal-clear to Delphine that everything was finished between us. My mistake was in telling her she could keep that confounded ring. She'd never given it back, of course, so I told her to sell it, do anything she liked with it. If I'd known what she had in mind, I'd have rammed the bloody thing down her throat.' He stroked her cheek. 'When she appeared out of the blue like that I could hardly believe her sheer brass-faced cheek.'

Sophie was beginning to feel better. 'I thought you were struck dumb by that incredible face of hers.'

Alexander's eyes lit suddenly with laughter. 'Turned to stone, you mean. Like one of those

Greeks faced with Medusa.'

'Then why did she come to warn me off, Alexander? She must have known I'd find out she was lying.'

He sighed heavily. 'Delphine's been spoiled all her life, given everything she wants simply because of the way she looks. Then suddenly she loses face twice in the space of a very short time, first with the job in the States, then with me. So she needed a whipping-boy. Someone she could vent her spite on.'

'And once again I was the nearest,' said Sophie wryly.

Alexander raised an eyebrow. 'Not at all. Delphine went berserk because I told her it was you wanted to marry, not her.'

She stared at him in dismay. 'But that isn't true!'

'Oh, yes, it is.' He leaned closer. 'You know very well you're going to marry me, Sophie.'

She pushed him away, and shrank back against the sofa cushions. 'I know nothing of the kind.'

'At the very moment Delphine interrupted us you were about to make me a very personal request. Am I right?' Alexander's eyes were steely with determination. 'Do you deny it?'

'No, I don't. But asking you to—to take me to bed doesn't mean I want to *marry* you, Alexander.'

He jumped to his feet, raking a hand through his hair as he glared down at her. 'You mean I'm OK for a quick session in bed, but otherwise on my bike!'

Sophie's head was beginning to throb. 'I don't know why you're so angry. Isn't that precisely what you had in mind before the window fell in?'

His face hardened. 'It's true I wanted to make
love to you. Enough to fight you tooth and nail to
do so, for my sins. But only because I meant to
show you it was you I wanted more than anything
or anyone in the world, including Delphine. To
make you see we belonged together, you and I,
Sophie. For life.'

Sophie was quite unable to cope with this on top
of the trauma of the night. 'Can we drop the
subject for now, Alexander? My head's thumping
so much I can't think.'

Alexander's tension drained from him, leaving
him very pale, with a look of weariness on his face
to match Sophie's. 'I'm sorry. I seem to keep on
saying that, don't I?' He rubbed a hand over his
face. 'I just felt I couldn't go on any longer without
clearing things up between us.'

'Thank you for that.' Sophie gave him a tired
smile. 'Come back when I've gathered my wander-
ing wits together.'

Alexander looked morose. 'Whatever you say,
Sophie. But in the meantime try to give my proposal some thought. Please.'

'It won't make any difference, Alexander,' she
felt obliged to point out. 'I told Delphine yesterday
that marriage had no place on my programme. I
meant it.'

Alexander's eyes glittered angrily in his ashen
face. 'I don't believe you.'

'That's your privilege, of course.' Sophie
shrugged. 'Believe this, at least, Alexander. If I
were marriage-inclined, you'd be the only husband

I'd want. But husbands rarely come as a single item. They're part of a package, along with children and cooking and laundry and housework. No novelty for me, any of it.'

'You haven't mentioned love.'

'Neither have you.'

There was a short, tense pause, while green eyes bored into brown, then Alexander turned away blindly and made for the door.

CHAPTER ELEVEN

SOPHIE was glad to spend the rest of the afternoon in bed, utterly worn out one way and another, but, deaf to Kate's entreaties, she insisted on getting up for dinner, and came downstairs to a house filled with flowers. There were carnations from Sam Jefford, a great glowing sheaf of chrysanthemums from Perry, and, last but by no means least, a very delicate arrangement of white violets and greenery from Julian Brett.

'Nice to be popular,' commented Dr Gordon.

'Must be easier ways to merit bouquets, Dad!' Sophie smiled cheerfully, secretly disappointed because none of the flowers were from Alexander. Which, she told herself sternly, was silly. He'd looked a lot worse than she did by the time he left. Certainly in no condition to think about flowers or anything else but getting himself home to bed.

Later in the evening there were several phone calls from friends who'd heard about the accident, including one from Sam Jefford, who was very sympathetic, but sensibly brief. She was touched by his concern, but a great deal less pleased when the doorbell rang and Julian Brett was ushered in. He told Sophie she looked quite dreadful, and went on to hold forth interminably on the evils and risks of girls living alone and unprotected. When

Sophie informed him he was mistaken, that in fact Alexander had been with her at the time, he looked deeply affronted, and only Perry's timely arrival prevented a further lecture. Julian approved of Perry even less than Alexander, and quickly took himself off, to Sophie's guilty relief.

'Right then, Perry,' she said urgently. 'How's the cottage?'

He cheered her up considerably by telling her that apart from a new window, and probably a new bedroom ceiling as well, Ilex Cottage was in reasonably good shape.

'Which is more than can be said for you, love,' he added. 'You look distinctly wan.'

'I feel wan!' Sophie grinned. 'So would you if a window had fallen on your head.'

Perry's blue eyes were quizzical. 'Lucky thing Alexander was on hand.'

Sophie flushed. 'Yes. Very.'

'Poor chap had a hell of a night. Once he knew you were all right he dashed back to Church Row to see if your neighbours were in need of help.'

Sophie put a hand to her mouth. 'My God, I never gave them a thought! Were they all right?'

'Startled by the commotion, and very worried about you, but otherwise unaffected.' Perry got up to go. 'Things better between you and Alexander now?'

'In a way.'

'Hm. Well, all I can say, love, is that Alexander was not exactly a ray of sunshine this afternoon.'

'This afternoon?' she said sharply. 'I thought he was going home to bed.'

'No, darling. He insisted on going back to Ilex Cottage with me to see the damage for himself. Then he bullied a glazier to replace the window at once, and organised a decorator to see to the plastering and paintwork in your bedroom. I rather fancy Alexander thinks the cottage means more to you than anything. Including him.' Perry bent to kiss her colourless cheek. 'Mrs Rogers has produced a niece who can fill in for you at the office for a few days. So don't think about coming back until you're well. Right?'

Sophie thanked Perry gratefully, then lay lost in thought once he was gone. So Alexander had checked over her cottage in person, after all; rather like heaping coals of fire on her ungrateful head.

'Cecily's been on the phone,' said Kate, coming in with a tea-tray. 'I said you were knee-deep in visitors, and suggested she came over for lunch tomorrow.'

Sophie thanked Kate affectionately, drank her tea then went back to bed. Rest, she decided, was essential one way and another, if she were to get back to work as quickly as possible, or even muster up sufficient stamina to hold her own against Alexander when he resumed the battle over their future relationship. *If* he renewed it.

Alexander made no move to do any such thing, Sophie found, feeling distinctly anticlimactic when his manner towards her was cheerfully friendly during his subsequent visits. These were brief, and no one would have suspected from his demeanour that his feelings towards his sibling-by-marriage were anything more than affectionate concern about her health. The latter improved daily. Sophie's temper did not. Her dressings gradually diminished in size, the stitches were removed from her scalp, the soreness and pain died away, and her appetite returned, nurtured lovingly by Kate. Still Alexander spent no more than a few minutes with Sophie at any one time. Some days he was unable to put in an appearance at all, and even when he did he somehow contrived never to be alone with her. Sophie began to wonder if the talk of marriage had been a hallucination, born of trauma and concussion. The Alexander who came with books and records as presents for the invalid was more fraternal towards her than her brothers themselves, since the twins' concern was limited to a phone call or two and an extremely vulgar get-well card. Sophie looked forward to her return to work, since it seemed likely she'd see more of Alexander at the office than she did at home with her father and Kate. But during the first few days back at her post she saw nothing of him at all, since he was away, and she was obliged to make do with second-hand accounts of his movements from Perry. Alexander, she concluded, had taken her at her word and decided to drop the subject of marriage. Or any other kind of relationship.

The prospect was so depressing that Sophie called in the Unicorn on the Friday lunch time to volunteer her services over the weekend, and the Mitchells, once satisfied Sophie was fully recovered, were gratifyingly eager to take advantage of the offer for Saturday evening. In spite of opposition from her father and Kate,

Sophie insisted on spending the night afterwards at Ilex Cottage on her sitting-room couch, since the bedroom was still recovering from the night of the storm. For the time being Kate was driving her to and from Deansbury each day, but Sophie had no intention of involving either Kate or her father in any social extras.

Dr Gordon took himself off for a rare round of golf at the weekend and Sophie spent Saturday morning shopping with Kate, then volunteered to make lunch, so that it was Kate who went off to answer the telephone when it rang.

'Alexander,' Kate mouthed silently, and whisked herself upstairs out of earshot.

'Sophie? How are you after your week at the office?'

Annoyed to find the mere sound of Alexander's voice affected her knees so badly, Sophie was extra cool with her assurances about her well-being.

'Then will you have dinner with me tonight, Sophie?'

She breathed in deeply. 'Sorry. I can't.'

'Can't? Or won't?'

'I already have an engagement,' she snapped, stung by the sarcasm in his voice. 'Not surprising, really, Alexander. It *is* the weekend.'

'I've been away for a couple of days. As you well know,' he added curtly.

'Yes, I do. Successful?'

'Never mind that.' Alexander sounded brusque and impatient. 'Can't you put off whoever you're tied up with tonight? I want to talk to you.'

'Sorry,' she cooed. 'Can't be done. Some other

time, perhaps.' She heard a loud click in her ear, then smiled, cat-like, as she put the phone down.

'You look very pleased with yourself,' observed Kate over lunch.

Sophie grinned. 'I am, rather. Alexander asked me out to dinner.'

Kate eyed her narrowly. 'I assume he wasn't overjoyed to learn you're working at the Unicorn.'

'I didn't tell him. He thinks I'm going out with someone else.'

Kate shook her head. 'I wish you two would sort yourselves out, you know. It's wearing to be in the same room with the pair of you these days.'

'You haven't been lately,' said Sophie tartly. 'Alexander's been conspicuous by his absence.'

'Ah! I see.'

Sophie scowled at her new stepmother blackly, then began to laugh. 'You think I'm behaving like a spoilt child.'

'No.' Kate smiled. 'Like a girl in love, Sophie.'

Saturday night was, not surprisingly, very busy at the Unicorn. Sophie was welcomed with open arms by the new girl who'd taken over behind the bar. Linda was tall and blonde and very good-natured, but, as she said to Sophie, she had only one pair of hands and feet, and even with mine host and his wife working at full stretch, extra help was a godsend.

For most of the evening Sophie coped very well, dealing pleasantly with the customers and doing her share of the chores. Then, towards nine, a lull enabled Frank Mitchell to go down to the cellar for

more soft drinks, and Sophie to round up the
empty glasses. The lounge bar was the haunt of
smart young couples, except for one large table
crammed with noisy young men celebrating the
home win of the local rugby team. As Sophie
collected a handful of tankards, the most present-
able of the group caught her round the waist,
grinning familiarly into her startled face.

'You're new, love. Haven't I seen you somewhere before?'

Loud brays of laughter from his companions
greeted the hoary approach, and Sophie did her
best to smile pleasantly as she removed herself
smartly from the young man's grasp.

'Trouble?' asked Anna Mitchell, as Sophie
returned to the bar.

'No. Harmless enough, I think.' But she was
glad to take the landlady's advice and remain
behind the bar, leaving Frank Mitchell to collect
glasses from then on.

Her Lothario, however, was undeterred. On his
way back from the men's cloakroom he elbowed
himself a place at the bar and remained there,
watching Sophie's every move during the time he
took to dispose of three pints of beer.

'Creepy,' said Linda in an undertone. 'One of
the Dawsons from Mile End House. Fancies his
chance with the girls.'

'Not with this one!' Sophie tried to ignore the
unswerving stare, but it was difficult, busy though
she was. Then she tried moving to the other end of
the bar, but her admirer promptly followed, thrust-
ing to a point of vantage as near to her as he could

get, waving a twenty-pound note under her nose.

'Give me a whisky this time, darling,' he said, smiling at Sophie with the confidence of someone who believed himself irresistible.

'Certainly, sir.' Sophie supplied the drink, took the note and gave him his change, counting it into his outstretched hand. Suddenly he caught her wrist.

'Can I drive you home later?'

Sophie shook her head, smiling pleasantly. 'Sorry.'

'Oh, come on, don't be shy.' He smiled cajolingly, his fingers tightening. 'Pretty girl like you shouldn't be shy.'

'Please excuse me—I have other customers to see to,' said Sophie, feeling her temper rise.

'S'all right with Frank. He knows me.' The man laughed. 'Everyone knows me. I'm Phil Dawson, from Mile End House.' It was an announcement expected to impress.

'How do you do?' Sophie pulled her hand away sharply, conscious of amused faces watching the little interplay, then hurried off, irritated. Her undismayed admirer stayed where he was, never taking his eyes off her, and refused to let anyone else serve him a drink.

'Humour him if you can,' said Frank Mitchell quietly. 'Don't worry. I'll see he doesn't get out of hand.'

Reluctantly Sophie supplied the persistent young man with a second whisky, and once more he captured her hand.

'You're cute,' he informed her.

'And you're beginning to bore me,' she retorted.
'Let go.'

'Now, now, don't be unfriendly, sweetheart.'
He was very flushed by this time, with a
dangerously belligerent look about him. 'Girls like
me,' he bragged loudly.

'Not this one!' Sophie tugged angrily, but he
hung on to her hand, his face turning ugly as he
realised she meant what she said.

Suddenly a familiar hand shot from behind to
close in a grip of iron on the unfortunate Mr
Dawson's wrist, and Sophie stared up in dismay at
the formidable sight of Alexander in a towering
rage.

'Who the hell are you?' blustered her unwanted
admirer.

'The lady's fiancé. Take your hands off her.
Now!'

Any protest the importunate Phil Dawson had in
mind died a very quick death as he saw the look in
the eyes of Sophie's rescuer.

'Just a bit of fun,' he muttered, and retreated
hastily, leaving Sophie to the full force of
Alexander's icy displeasure.

'I've had a word with Frank Mitchell. You're
coming with me. Now. Get your coat,' said
Alexander very quietly.

Sophie opened her mouth to protest.

'If you don't,' he said, forestalling her, 'I shall
come round there and carry you out bodily.'

It was patently clear Alexander meant what he
said. Sophie took leave of the Mitchells and Linda,
then collected her coat and followed Alexander to

the car park at the back of the Unicorn. In fraught silence she slid into the car as he held the door open for her.

'You had no business to do that,' she said coldly, deciding to carry the war into the enemy's camp as he started the car.

'I disagree. Unless, of course, you enjoy being pawed by all and sundry.'

Sophie decided to ignore this. 'How did you know where I was?'

'I went to see Kate and your father.' Alexander gave her a cold, sidelong look. 'I learnt that this isn't the first time you've worked at the Unicorn. And that David is no happier about it than I am.'

'But he, of course, being a man of reason, realises I'm adult and able to do what I like with my life, whether it's working in a pub or living on my own.' Sophie stared stonily through the windscreen.

Alexander made no reply. He drove in taut silence, swiftly and skilfully, as always, until they reached Brading and the high hedges of Willow Reach. Sophie kept up her silence stubbornly as she slid out of the car, disdaining his helping hand as she stalked ahead of him.

'I thought you'd like to see the place now it's finished,' said Alexander neutrally, as he unlocked the door.

Sophie's anger began to recede almost as soon as she put foot inside the house. There was something in the atmosphere of Willow Reach which made her anger and resentment seem unnecessary, and almost against her will she felt her defiance dissolve. The peace and tranquillity of the house was a tangible thing, something she could almost reach out and touch as she walked with Alexander through the graceful, uncluttered rooms, gazing at the harmony their mutual blend of taste had achieved. She was shaken badly by a fierce pang of possessiveness, and subsided on one of the sofas in the drawing-room, a prey to emotions she shied from analysing.

'It's beautiful, Alexander. Perfect.'

He sat beside her, turning sardonic eyes on her pensive face. 'Beautiful, yes. Perfect, no.'

'Oh, I know it's not fully furnished yet——'

'I meant it's not a house for a man to live in alone. No, hear me,' he said, as Sophie would have spoken. 'It's strange,' he went on. 'I altered the Chantry for Delphine, because she thought it was so smart to turn an old house into the kind of showplace you see in magazines. Yet afterwards there was no mark of her personality there. Nor oddly enough, of me, although I'd lived there all my life and designed the alterations myself. In fact, when I visit Kate and David there now, it's *their* house already. So much so I might never have been there at all.'

'But *this* house is yours,' said Sophie. She twisted the gold signet ring on her little finger, not looking at him. 'This is your creation, isn't it? Your brain-child. The other occupants were almost like caretakers, in a way. Just keeping it ready for you to take over one day.'

Alexander nodded. 'Exactly. And the fact that you understand so well only underlines what I'm about to say.'

Sophie stiffened. 'Alexander——' she began, but he reached out and put a finger on her lips.

'Let me finish, Sophie. Please.'

She subsided, her pulse racing at his touch.

'Don't look so tense, Sophie,' he said gently. 'I just thought you'd like to know the house is haunted.'

'By the mistress of your Restoration courtier?'

'No. One can be haunted by events from the future, not just the past.' Alexander moved until he was near enough to take her hand. 'In this house I'm haunted by you, Sophie, by a vision of how it would be if we were here together, sharing our lives.' He took her by the shoulders, turning her towards him. 'We happen to have arrived at this juncture in the opposite direction from most people, Sophie. We've known each other so well all our lives, we never saw what was under our noses all the time.'

'How can I believe that when you almost married Delphine?' said Sophie urgently. 'And the "almost" bit is due to *her*—not you. If Terry Foyle hadn't arrived that day to tempt Delphine to the States, you'd be a much married man by now.'

'And regretting it.' A look of distaste shadowed Alexander's face, then he smiled. 'Funny, really. Terry Foyle, unknown to himself, will always have my undying gratitude.'

'If we—we did get married,' said Sophie with care, 'how do you know you might not repent in haste over me, too?'

Alexander drew her very gently into his arms.

'Because we've done all the other part, Sophie. We know each other better than some couples learn to do all their lives. You've worked with me, known me at my worst, God knows, and hopefully at my best, too.' He put a finger under her chin and lifted her face up to his. 'All that's left is to become lovers. Would that be so difficult?'

'You know only too well how easy it would be.' Sophie looked up into his intent face. 'Which leads me to ask for my own say, Alexander. Before you go any further I'd like to put forward a proposition of my own.'

Alexander looked rather as though she'd thrown a bucket of water in his face. 'What is it?' he asked warily.

Sophie took in a deep breath. 'You know how I feel about domesticity. I'm no career woman, I grant you that, but I enjoy my job and if I have to carry on with it all my working life I'll be perfectly happy. You see, now, for the first time ever, I've got a place of my own, a life of my own, with no one to consider but me. And I love it, Alexander.'

He jerked away, jumping to his feet. 'Then there's no more to be said.'

'No, wait! You hear me out this time.' Sophie hesitated, then blurted, 'Couldn't I just be your mistress, Alexander?'

He swung round in utter astonishment. 'My *what?*'

'Your mistress,' she said resolutely, feeling her colour rise. 'I mean, you could spend your evenings with me, or as many of them as you wanted. Nights, too, if you like. Weekends in

London, maybe, or even Paris. Holidays. That sort of thing.'

Alexander stared at her as though she'd lost her wits. He raked a hand through his hair, then his lips began to twitch uncontrollably and he dissolved into laughter.

Sophie glared at him. 'What's so funny?'

Alexander breathed deeply, trying hard to control himself. 'I had this vision of myself slinking up to your door to find you reclining on that chaise-longue in a—a négligé, is that right? All seduction and suspenders!' He bit his lip hard. 'My *mistress,* for God's sake! What put that idea in your head?'

'If you're going to make a great big joke about it——' she began huffily, and jumped up, but Alexander caught her, holding her loosely round the waist.

'Sorry. I couldn't help it, Sophie. It's such a preposterous idea.'

'Lots of people don't get married these days,' she said sulkily.

'But they usually live together, nitwit! A mistress is something a *married* man indulges himself in, darling. If he can afford it.'

They looked at each other in silence for a moment, while Sophie's flaring colour faded.

'I love you, Sophie,' said Alexander unsteadily. 'I want you here with me. Always. I don't relish the thought of snatched hours of illicit bliss, thank you just the same, bliss though they'd certainly be. I don't fancy sneaking along Church Row in the small hours, hoping Mrs Perkins wouldn't see me.

I want a wife. I want *you*.'

'But I had everything worked out so beautifully,' wailed Sophie in desperation. 'It all seemed to be *meant*. I mean, Gran finding me the cottage, the new Paget branch opening up in Arlesford just as the job with Sam Jefford fell through . . .' She trailed away, eyeing him with suspicion. 'That's a very odd look.'

Alexander's eyes flickered, then he sighed. 'Let's sit down, Sophie.'

She looked at him in alarm, but allowed him to settle her in the crook of his arm on the sofa again.

'Sophie, did you learn about my namesake in school?' he said unexpectedly.

Sophie frowned, surprised. 'Of course. Alexander the Great. Julian calls you that when he's feeling bitchy.'

Alexander snorted. 'He would! Anyway, brought it up because I'm trying to explain something to you. If you remember, a certain Phrygian king by the name of Gordius tied a complicated knot no one could unravel, until Alexander came along with his sword and simply cut the Gordian knot in half.'

Sophie nodded, mystified. 'So?'

'I feel we've rather got ourselves tied up in the same sort of knot, so I'm going to wield a figurative sword to *un*tie it. In a way I've done it before on your behalf. You see I haven't always been wrapped up in my own problems, even during the time I was involved with Delphine. I knew better than anyone how much you longed to leave home like the boys. So when my tenants in Ilex Cottage left——'

'*Your* tenants?' Sophie's eyes opened wide.

'Yes. It belongs to me. So I told Cecily you could have it for a while. Until you got married.' His smile was rueful. 'Only I didn't realise at the time I meant until you were married to me.'

Sophie's eyes dulled to a forlorn, lost look. 'So Ilex Cottage was yours all the time.'

His arm tightened. 'There's a bit more, too. I'd better come clean and tell you one of the reasons I made Arlesford my choice for the branch office was so you could work for me there.'

'But—but I was all set to work for Sam Jefford!'

'I did a deal with him. If he told you the job was off, I'd put as much work his way as I could, on top of the branch office, the sale of your house, and so on.'

Sophie pushed away his arm and jumped to her feet, pacing back and forth in the space between the sofas. 'So,' she said tightly, 'all this new life of mine wasn't mine at all. I got it by courtesy of Alexander Paget.'

He nodded, his eyes shuttered. 'In a way. I wanted to keep you in my ken. Somewhere I could keep an eye on you.'

'Big Brother!' she said bitterly. 'As if I didn't have enough brothers of my own.'

Alexander rose to his feet and caught her by the hands. 'I'm not your brother, Sophie. I want to be your lover, your husband. *And,*' he added forcefully, 'contrary to your belief, it *is* possible for a man to be both.'

Sophie turned her head away sharply, trying to come to terms with the cold new light shining on her bid for independence. What a farce it had all been, she thought bitterly, her teeth sinking so hard into her bottom lip that they drew blood. At last she looked up into his watchful face, with a smile that stopped short of her eyes.

'All right, Alexander. You win. Now I think I'd like to go home, please.'

His eyes narrowed. 'You mean you *will* marry me?'

'I suppose so. If Ilex Cottage belongs to you, it's pretty pointless my staying there. I might as well move in here and let you rent it out again, save you some money. And since you're so set on a conventional arrangement, all right. Let's get married.'

Alexander pulled her into his arms. 'You haven't said anything about feelings, Sophie. I thought you'd be angry with me, God knows, but I'd prefer a tantrum to apathy. *Do* you love me?'

She shrugged. 'I'm not sure.'

'Then why the hell are you marrying me?'

'Because if I don't, I assume your fine Italian hand will be writing the script for the rest of my life anyway,' she cut back at him, suddenly fierce. 'Whatever I do, wherever I try to go—there you are, blocking my way. So to hell with it. Let's get married. I give in.'

Alexander flushed, then paled, his eyes glittering like a cat's in his set face, and suddenly he gave a smothered curse and took her by the hand, pulling her along with him as he strode from the room and up the stairs to the master bedroom at the front of the house.

'What are you going to do?' Sophie panted, as he kicked the door shut behind them. 'Careful—you'll mark the wood!'

'What do you think I'm going to do?' he said through clenched teeth. 'I'm sure as hell not marrying a female whose only reason for saying yes is because she's given up saying no. So I think I'll take advantage of your original offer. Once, anyway.'

'Not like this,' wailed Sophie miserably, as she found herself dumped in the middle of the bed. 'Please, Alexander!'

'Shut up.' And Alexander silenced her protests in the most effective way possible, stifling them with his mouth as he began removing her clothes.

'I don't——' she gasped, pushing at him.

'Yes, you do,' he said flatly, and began to caress her breasts, her stomach, moving to her thighs as his mouth left hers to rove all over her, everywhere, astounding her by its encroachment on parts of her she had never dreamed would be so clamorous in response. The audacity of his marauding tongue took her breath away, and she stiffened as it left her navel to move downwards.

'No!' she cried, rearing up, but he pushed her flat and parted her unwilling thighs to find the place that pulsed with response to his tongue.

'No!' she said hoarsely, almost sobbing, her head thrashing to and fro. 'No—no——' But the words ended in a choked, quavering moan as waves of hot, languorous sensation convulsed her body. Before she had time to recover Alexander moved swiftly, and almost before the throbbing had subsided he was over her and inside her and she gasped at their merging, her body rigid for a moment before it yielded. Abandoning all effort at resistance, Sophie clutched at Alexander as her one constant in an earthquake of new sensation as he swept her along on a mad, careering ride to the final glory they experienced almost in unison.

Afterwards they lay very still for a long, silent interval while their pulses steadied and their breathing slowed, and Sophie came to terms with a fact she'd suspected all along. It would be very nice indeed to be mistress to a lover of Alexander's calibre. After years of Julian's company it was reassuring to find that a man like Alexander could want her so badly.

'What are you thinking about?' asked Alexander at last, moving so that she fitted snugly against him.

'Julian.'

'*What?*' Alexander shot up in outrage, but she pulled him down to her again. He allowed her to soothe him, then turned her towards him so that they lay eye to eye, one of his legs thrown over hers in an intimacy which distracted Sophie very thoroughly from thoughts of any other man.

'I always thought Julian Brett's preference was not inclined in a feminine direction,' said Alexander bluntly. 'I could never see why you bothered with him.'

'Convenience. And I was his cover, I suppose.' Sophie smiled into the eyes so close to hers. 'Julian is one of those men who is just plain celibate, Alexander. Not gay. Once upon a time a man could be a bachelor without comment, but these days it's different. So we had a sort of tacit arrangement. He wined me and dined me fairly regularly. In return I had a man in my life I knew wouldn't get any ideas about marriage.'

'Like me.'

'Nobody's like you, Alexander. Mind you,' added Sophie, 'he did propose some sort of marriage when I told him I was moving away. Said I could move in with him and his mother—that I'd be company for her.'

Alexander shook with laughter against her. 'As proposals go, surely mine's more tempting than that.' He ran the tip of his finger over her lips and Sophie bit it gently.

'Very true. In fact——' She paused, wriggling even closer. 'I've changed my mind again about marriage.'

Alexander lay very still. 'You mean it's no now, not yes?'

'No, I mean it's yes now, not no.' Sophie giggled. 'If you see what I mean.'

'Elucidate,' he said sternly, then held her so tightly that Sophie was reassured enough to comply.

'Perhaps,' she said slowly, 'marriage to you wouldn't be so bad, after all.'

'Careful, Sophie. Much more flattery like that and I'll get above myself!'

She kicked his ankle. 'What I *meant* was that, here with you like this, I feel I could very much enjoy being married to you, Alexander.'

'Why, thank you, Sophie. Does that mean I pass muster as a lover?'

'As I've always said, Alexander, superior's the

word.' She thought for a moment. 'No. I've
changed my mind. Incomparable is better.'

Alexander kissed her deeply, his hand moving
down her spine to press her closer against him. He
raised his head a fraction to smile into her eyes. 'A
graceful compliment,' he whispered. 'Except that
comparison isn't possible, is it, darling? I'm the first
lover you've ever had.'

'True.'

'I'm going to be the first husband you've ever
had, too. And the last. Agreed?' He kissed her
hard. 'And I'll be a good husband, I promise.'

She chuckled. 'You'll be a *great* husband—
Alexander!'

'No corny jokes, please!' He turned her over on
her back and hung over her. 'But I've had a great
idea.'

'Really?' she said, breathless.

'Since—for some reason—you appear to have
changed your mind about marriage——'

'You seduced me into it!'

'Do you mind?'

'No.'

'Right. Now because, like my namesake, my
strategy was so brilliant that you capitulated——'

'Is that what I've done?' She ran her hand down
his thigh, and he breathed in sharply.

'More or less. To proceed, since you are now
more amenable to the prospect of our legal union,
I'm prepared to make concessions.'

'Such as?'

'I'm prepared to get someone to help you with the
housework you detest so much, I'll even cook

dinner myself sometimes—after all, the greatest chefs are men—ouch! Don't be so violent. Then, when we send the children——'

'What children?'

'Ours. I repeat, when our children go to school I'll persuade Kate to sew on their name tapes!' Alexander grinned down at her in such smug triumph that Sophie gave him a great dig in the ribs, whereupon he tickled her in retaliation and they collapsed together, helpless with laughter which gradually gave way to something very different as Alexander proceeded to demonstrate, beyond any last possible doubt Sophie might have harboured, how very superior a lover he could be when given the right and proper encouragement. If proper was the word.

Especially for you,
Christmas from
HARLEQUIN HISTORICALS

An enchanting collection of three Christmas
stories by some of your favorite authors captures
the spirit of the season in the 1800s

TUMBLEWEED CHRISTMAS by Kristin James

A "Bah, humbug" Texas rancher meets his match in his
new housekeeper, a woman determined to bring the spirit
of a Tumbleweed Christmas into his life—and love into
his heart.

A CINDERELLA CHRISTMAS by Lucy Elliot

The perfect granddaughter, sister and aunt, Mary Hillyer
seemed destined for spinsterhood until Jack Gates arrived
to discover a woman with dreams and passions that were
meant to be shared during a Cinderella Christmas.

HOME FOR CHRISTMAS
by Heather Graham Pozzessere

The magic of the season brings peace Home For
Christmas when a Yankee captain and a Southern heiress
fall in love during the Civil War.

HIST-XMAS-1R

Wonderful, luxurious gifts can be yours with proofs-of-purchase from any specially marked "Indulge A Little" Harlequin or Silhouette book with the Offer Certificate properly completed, plus a check or money order (do not send cash) to cover postage and handling payable to Harlequin/Silhouette "Indulge A Little, Give A Lot" Offer. We will send you the specified gift.

Mail-in-Offer

| | OFFER CERTIFICATE | | | |
Item:	A. Collector's Doll	B. Soaps in a Basket	C. Potpourri Sachet	D. Scented Hangers
# of Proofs-of -Purchase	18	12	6	4
Postage & Handling	$3.25	$2.75	$2.25	$2.00
Check One				

Name _____

Address _____ Apt. # _____

City _____ State _____ Zip _____

ONE PROOF OF PURCHASE

To collect your free gift by mail you must include the necessary number of proofs-of-purchase plus postage and handling with offer certificate.

HP-3

Harlequin®/Silhouette®

Mail this certificate, designated number of proofs-of-purchase and check or money order for postage and handling to:

INDULGE A LITTLE
P.O. Box 9055
Buffalo, N.Y. 14269-9055